HOMO COSMICUS

A Science Fiction Novel

by Todor Bombov

Strategic Book Publishing and Rights Co.

Strategic Book Publishing and Rights Co., LLC
USA | Singapore
www.sbpra.net

For information about special discounts for bulk purchases, please contact Strategic Book Publishing and Rights Co. Special Sales, at bookorder@sbpra.net.

ISBN: 978-1-946540-04-1

Book Design: Suzanne Kelly

I dedicate this book to my precious princess Nady, who, I hope, will live in a better and nicer world.

PREFACE

The sci-fi novel *Homo Cosmicus* was written during the entire year of 1990 and was completed at year's end. The idea to write this book was provoked by the CNN global contest, "What vision do you have on the development of the world after 30 years?" It wasn't noticed then; maybe it wasn't written well then. In 2002, I succeeded in publishing the book in my country of Bulgaria, after some cosmetic changes.

In the second half of 2013, I was already concerned with the translation of this book when I watched the episodes with the fantabulous magician, Steven Frayne, known by his artistic name, Dynamo. He made effortless performances of all the miracles of Jesus, from walking on water to the resurrection itself! I was deeply impressed! Of course, Dynamo was a brilliant conjuror who had a brilliant team. All of them together made those wonderful illusions. But I saw with my eyes that all the forecasts I had written in this book far before seeing him, all my prognostications from 1990 about a society in the not-so-distant future, will be true. Yes, they will happen! Here, on this Earth! With only the power of his mind, this future man will be able to master such miracles as telepathy, levitation, and even rainbow body phenomenon and teleportation. It's clear to me that a man born by woman could turn into a living god. What Dynamo demonstrated to us as illusions, as magic—transforming his body into a tool as a means of the mind (from water heater to magnet, as the occasion requires)—all of this will be a way of normal life of this future man. I'm deeply convinced that after only a few centuries, a new society of several billion people will have such a way of life.

Another prediction in this book that I wrote back in 1990 has already come true—the appearance of the *infeneric money*, energy-information money! Well, from 2009 we saw only half of it—the cybernetic part; its energy part could well appear in the future. In 1990 I called this currency *biterg*, now it is known as bitcoin. But the evolution of money has still not ended. The current cryptocurrencies are only a stage of an eventual transformational development of the monetary system wherein these cryptocurrencies in the future would be really transformed into energy-information money, into infeneric money. But the staple topic in this book is a society without money! A perfect society without the State, too! That means, however, in order to attain this perfection in and for every member of society, the very society itself must attain perfection! How? Just read!

1

January 1989

"What a wonderful night, Umberto!"

"Yes, sure, it just enchants. Just look up at this sky!"

The night in this northern region of Chile was always especially clear beneath the fathomless vault of heaven. But because of the new moon, it was now merely pellucid and pure, as if one could drink by it. The night was cold and unusually black with multiple clusters of big crystal stars that seemed carelessly spilled and scattered by someone in all possible directions. Of course, in open and level country like this in the desert, the stars' visibility was just perfect. One had the feeling that he could gather them with cupped hands if only his hands could stretch that far.

The two soldiers, Umberto Rojas and Pedro Rosales, were at their post and, from time to time, tossed some word between them in order to while away the hours. It was almost at the half-way point of their guard duty, and they had to keep themselves alert to watch yet another hour just as it became perhaps the most sleepy time—four o'clock. The soldiers, who were on military patrol, were overtaken by the night here in this open place. Their five other comrades-in-arms were lying down around the fire, which was kept going all night, and sleeping soundly. A little aside from them lay their commander Corporal Armando Valdes. The corporal was also fast asleep. All around was so quiet and calm that nothing foreboded what would occur next.

Suddenly, as they absently roved a look around them in the dark, both of the guards were instantly stupefied, frozen as if they'd been dug into the ground. For vaguely short time, in front of their eyes, emerged from the sky some strange solids, diffusing neon light all around. The objects settled on the ground a respectable distance from them. Just for a few twinkles, as if from the nonentity, from the nothingness, they descended and became as two stars, enlarging their dimensions to enormous orbs, whereupon a smaller light-sphere detached from the bigger one and quite unexpectedly touched down onto the ground only about a hundred yards from the watching young men, startled and struck dumb as stone statues. In their mortal fear they instinctively joined hands. All occurred so quickly and quietly that they were not sure whether they suffered from hallucinations—these two mysterious specters, like glass pearls in ultramarine, stood there like a night phantasm from an ill-omened haunt of ghosts.

Pedro Rosales winced in fear and stampeded to the corporal. When the soldier was waking him up, feverish and all in a fluster, he looked quite accidentally and unconsciously at the watch on his superior's wrist. The corporal, boggled by the wild, jerky impulse of his soldier, rose to his feet, drowsy and cross. He also looked at the time. It was 4 o'clock and 15 minutes. Very quickly, however, he understood that the soldier had a right to wake him up. Not far from them, two brightly luminous violet globes mutely stood side by side. The violet light made them unusually beautiful and at the same time mysteriously sinister. There was something inexplicable about them, something simultaneously attractive and repulsive, something divine and demonic.

As the patrol's commander, Armando Valdes was under an obligation to understand what in fact these "guests" represented. He started to reconnoiter what kind of lights they were, but as soon as he went only a few yards, he suddenly just disappeared right before the eyes of his soldiers, all of whom were now standing and staring. Corporal Armando Valdes himself merely sank abruptly into the dark, absorbed in some invisible power of attraction.

The minutes ticked away slowly, so slowly that the seven soldiers stood in suspense, waiting what might befall them at any moment. This waiting made them all nervous. Five minutes went by, but the corporal was not back yet. The tension built up, but nobody ventured to start looking for Valdes. Perhaps the soldiers were paralyzed with fear right where they stood and could not stir even a foot forward. They only threw faint-hearted glances at each other from time to time while remaining quite silent.

Thus passed ten minutes or so of harassing suspense. Their eyes swam from staring such a long time, but the young men succeeded in noting that around each of the luminous spheres a thin crimson band turned slowly, very similar to the belt that girdled Saturn.

It seemed fifteen minutes or so had passed when Corporal Valdes both suddenly disappeared and re-appeared several yards from the jittery soldiers. The two foreigners continued to stand there as imperturbably and quietly as before, radiating their *calming*, soft, and pleasant violet light. This invisible and elusive power which was coming from them had, a little while ago, taken in—or rather *swallowed*—the commander of the military patrol. Now it was as if it had *spat* him back out. Valdes could hardly stand on his legs; he was all atremble and shook all over; he walked ahead with great effort, like an exhausted drowned man after a long skirmish with the elements of the sea. At once, the soldiers clamped around him to help and support him. Valdes was trying to say something, but his voice came out somehow hollow and alien, not his own normal voice. With a strange and most alien voice and still out of his senses, he faltered, looking out concentrated somewhere beyond the others:

"You don't know who we are and where we came from, but we'll be back soon!"

And he lapsed into silence. The soldiers all exchanged fearful glances. In the next moment, as if at an order, they all turned around to look at their night visitors but nobody was there. The *violets* had vanished. And no one had sensed them leave.

The corporal looked wretched. Valdes, always calm and vainly clean-shaven—he had nearly a week's stubble on his chin now—was so wrinkled and shabby, and his face so scrubby that he looked as though he had really struggled with some wild element. Then someone noticed that Valdes's wristwatch had stopped and was pointed to four o'clock and thirty minutes. This time coincided with his return time, because, in that moment, it was already four o'clock and thirty-two minutes. But there was something which, to put it mildly, confused the mind, something quite puzzling. The date section of the watch indicated five days ahead! This was a shaking and depressing fact, because it fit the corporal's current appearance. Valdes had lived five days, while for the others only fifteen minutes had passed! This was a shock! His metabolism had obviously been artificially accelerated in an unknown way. The question was whether the clock's time stopping and the date's turning were accidental circumstances? That might be the case except for all the other indicators: if his condition in that moment was normal, if this drama was not being played out in front of all of them. The boys asked questions; they talked spiritedly and noisily about the incident. Valdes, however, could not remember what had happened to him during those fifteen minutes—or maybe five days? He began slowly to recover himself only when he found himself near the fire; it was as if its life-giving warmth streamed into his tormented body. He was gradually coming to his senses but was feeling somehow very strange. The corporal was so horrified by the event which had befallen him that when he collected his faculties, but still living with his nightmare, he first began to yell for his mother. This whole incident was so inexplicable, unpleasant, and freakish. Various questions poured toward all sides of Valdes.

"What happened, Corporal, sir?"

"What's the matter?"

"How did you disappear?"

"What have you seen there?"

"Good Lord!" cried Valdes. "What was this? Can anybody explain it to me? ... I'd like to know what happened to me during these fifteen minutes. ... I'm ready, if it is needed, to be in a hypnotic state if only it could draw from my memory information about the incident. I don't remember anything!"

Day was dawning. The first streaks of light would soon beam across the horizon. The nocturnal nightmare, however, did not leave the small group but held all of the men still very troubled and mixed-up.

At the same this time, however, higher in the lightening sky the two night specters parted—one started towards the north-west, the other towards the north-east.

Less than a minute later, the enormous distance between South America and North America was surmounted. Here the night still reigned. A Pan American Airlines Boeing 707 was on its regular run from Houston to Detroit, flying at thirty-thousand feet. It was seventy-five miles out from Indianapolis. All was running normally until the moment when the copilot, Davis, looking at his part of the sky, noticed from the right and upward a big star that was not twinkling. But it was not a star; it was a yellow speckle drawn in at the ends. It stayed there, as though fixed on the spot.

"Miracles are few and far between," he reassured himself, without taking the thing he had seen seriously into consideration. "Maybe it's a refraction of light in the atmosphere, or … who knows what?"

What it did next, however, cut across any human notions about a miracle! From the speckle, a thread of light cropped out that shot straight downwards onto the ground.

"Look, Mike! See up there up! What is this?" cried Davis.

The flight mechanic, just glancing out from behind the board, at once suggested, "Captain, we must report it to air-traffic control!"

The descending thread of light suddenly enlarged, turning into a bright cone of light. From this moment on, all of the crew watched what was happening outside. A second cone of light appeared—wider but paler than the first. And after that descended, yet a third one, quite pale.

"Wait!" The captain threw his hands up in astonishment. "What can I report? We have to see what happens next. And what could this all be?"

No one knows better than pilots that a distance is hard to estimate by sight. In spite of that, all present had the same feeling that the unidentified object hung above Earth at approximately twenty-five or thirty miles! The copilot began feverishly to outline on a sheet of paper the image of the unusual phenomenon. Incredibly, in the sector of the earth lit up by the cone-shaped shaft of light, all was clearly seen—houses, roads, farms—as if in broad daylight! What emissive and concentrated power would this *spotlight* have to have in order to illuminate everything on Earth's surface in such minute detail from an altitude of thirty miles?

This spectacle did not last long. The *spotlight* switched off for a while, and the spectacle went on in Act Two. After the shaft of light was withdrawn for serial time, it was descended downwards again, but this time the *spotlight* rose right off Earth and tilted up, advancing towards the airplane.

Then the pilots saw a glaring white dot, and around it, concentrated colored circles. The captain still hesitated whether or not to report the occurrence. But suddenly something happened that put an end to all his doubt. The white dot suddenly flared up and, in its stead, a small, oval, greenish-blue cloud appeared.

"It switched on the engines and disappeared," said the copilot, who put involuntarily the phenomenon on the same footing as aviator's ordinary life.

And it seemed to Douglas, the captain, that the unearthly stranger had begun to draw nearer with an incredible velocity, cutting off the airliner's course under an acute angle. In short, the *bolide* started obliquely to intercept their course. Then Douglas shouted to the navigator, "Adams, report this to air-traffic control! Now!"

But—strange coincidence—after navigator Adams's first words, the object came to a sudden stop! It was as if it had caught the signals that were being sent to the air-traffic control and reacted immediately by stopping.

The air-traffic controller in Indianapolis took the crew's message only as a piece of information and quite politely, with feigned, schooled and even trained civility, and explained that, unfortunately, he himself did not see anything, neither on the radar screen nor in the sky.

"You see?" Davis took offence. "They'll say that we're insane. They'll probably call us unhinged!"

The greenish-blue, small cloud became more pronouncedly blue. All of a sudden, it sharply descended downwards past the airliner's altitude. After that, also quite abruptly, it swept up vertically. It flopped left and right, and then once again down and up, as though made of elastic, and it finally stopped dead just against the Boeing, fixing its height. The phantom had begun to fly along with the plane at thirty thousand feet altitude and five hundred miles per hour, as though bound to it and accompanying it in its flight.

"An escort of honor," Douglas rumbled out, "as a diplomatic corps!"

All the men fixed their gazes to the right. The new-comer flew imperturbably not far off from them, as if it was an invisibly bound satellite. Inside it, small *fires* started to coruscate across it, switching on and off like Christmas-tree lights or illuminated signs. They were followed by other ones which swarmed horizontally as small, scarlet fiery tongues in the middle of the craft. The most singular, the most enigmatic thing, however, was that this intruder, this *suito*r, had no metal outer casing! It had no steel sheath! It seemed rather to be made of some huge, crushed crystal.

The navigator conscientiously communicated all things the crew was seeing to the air-traffic control. In reply, all the crew heard the excited voice of the air-traffic controller:

"I see strays on the horizon! Where do you see your small cloud?"

The navigator answered.

"It coincides!" the controller noisily drawled.

The satellite began quite unexpectedly to show an unusual bearing and to take queer shapes. In front of the amazed eyes of the pilots, it grew a *tail*, resembling a tornado in shape—wide above, thin below. It formed a *comma*. After that, the *tail* began to rise upwards in the horizon, while the small cloud transformed from elliptical to quadrangular form.

"Look," the copilot chimed in, "it provokes us! It mocks us! Is it joking with us?"

Really, the plane was now escorted by a keen-prow *cloudy plane*—without wings, with a curled-up tailpiece and poured over in blue light. Where the nozzle is located in actual airplanes, it was in a difficult-to-see spot on this craft, as if it was some compact kernel.

Just at this moment of dramatic, exciting minutes, of supreme moments of tension, the cabin's door opened. It was the stewardess.

"Sir, the passengers are highly alarmed. They're asking what that thing is that has been flying next to the plane for some time now. What I should tell them, sir?"

All the men exchanged glances. Obviously, they were not the only spectators of this md-air garish spectacle of some conjuror showing them his best tricks. Douglas clenched his teeth weakly, thoughtfully scratched his stubbly beard, raised his eyes to the stewardess, and, delaying his answer, drew out his reply, almost like spelling it out.

"Susan, tell them that these are gleams cast back from the city's lights. Explain to them that it's an atmospheric phenomenon, static electricity, mirage, by jingo, even Northern Lights if you want, or something like that, which has always appeared at this time and at this height. Give them a lecture on optics, a lesson on reflection and refraction of light if it's needed—you know best. Just don't raise a panic!"

The stewardess went out.

"It seems it means no ill to us, sir," inserted the navigator.

"Yes, it seems like that. But how long until it will annoy us?"

During that time, in the radar zone of the dispatcher down in Indianapolis, entered another Boeing that flew from Detroit opposite the Houston's crew. The distance between the two planes was about sixty miles. It was impossible from such a distance not to spot the enormous *cloudy plane*.

In a moment, when the contact was established, the captain ordered, "Ask them whether they can locate this marvel!"

"They laugh, sir. They think us mad," Adams replied after a while.

"Well, leave it to me."

In response to Douglas's question, the captain of the Boeing flying from the opposite direction told Douglas that he was not seeing anything. The air-traffic controller in Indianapolis, who now was seeing the *cloudy plane* quite well, conveyed to Detroit's crew its coordinates and the direction where they should find the unusual phenomenon. But Detroit's Boeing pilots were literally like blind men. They were not seeing anything in the airspace in front of them; they could find nothing; no device in their cockpit could register anything unusual. With just about thirty miles to the meeting of the two planes, they began to see it and, with coinciding accuracy, they too described the plane-satellite which was floating like a specter, like some ghost, like a new *Flying Dutchman.*

Houston's plane flew over Fort Wayne and Toledo, accompanied by its illusory double, and the air-traffic controllers in these towns consecutively fixed the queer tandem. The tenacious chaser carrying out its cortege for hundreds of miles had already aroused the curiosity of too many people. Flying past Lake Erie, Captain Douglas's crew managed to estimate the dimensions of this *holographic* copy of their Boeing. The joint flight went on to Detroit whereupon the plane-shadow disappeared in an unknown direction.

2

Mr Manfred Böhme, well-known European physicist, had scarcely arisen and taken his morning cup of coffee out slack onto the garden lounge. He was there holidaying far away from the cold of his native North, where severe winter now blew. Rio was not only a rich, cosmopolitan city, but also a unique experience with all its provocations and temptations—a deep azure sky over a multitude of insular hills buried in greenery; long, wide beaches with fine golden or white sands; and exotic verdure inland from the coast. Rio, its emerald-blue sea with foamy waves and the sunny long days bathed in a yellow-crimson glow at dusk, days tinted in hues of blood and old gold at sunset. Rio, its nights suffused with lights; nights of all colors of the spectrum; nights of magic, music, and dances.

Manfred Böhme's villa was situated not far from the coast with a bewitching view where it caught clearly the sounds and smells of the ever-pleasant, calming surf.

The physicist was quietly sitting in his garden, feasting his eyes on all the beauties around, while swaying lightly in his rocking chair. The steward offered him the morning newspaper. Böhme was not carried away by cheap sensations but was intrigued simply by the ordinary human curiosity of a resting man as his eyes were riveted on the large letters in the paper before him: "UFO—myth or reality?" There had been three supposed sightings the preceding day. In the first message from Brazil, it maintained that two lads, students, had been abducted by a UFO on January 20. Manuel Roberto had been found in Rondonopolis on the next day, January 21, three hundred miles from his home, and he could not explain what had happened with his cousin, Paulo. He seemed rather stricken by all that he had seen and managed to remember.

The second report was about some Chilean corporal who had experienced a paralyzing stress, a genuine psychological shock during his contact with the extraterrestrials. They engendered similar complicated emotions in a US airliner's crew, which had been accompanied hundreds of miles by a strange solid with changing form that showed no aggression toward it. Some commentary followed.

Manfred Böhme looked through other news, too, and set down the newspaper. But something made him reach for it again. He found an interesting fact. The physicist took up paper and a ballpoint pen and, just for fun, began to reckon up something. But bit by bit he went deeper and this work engrossed him so much that he did not notice the approach of his friend, Francisco Gomes, who lived in the neighborhood and visited him during his sojourns.

"Good morning, Manfred. What are these calculations? Would you tell me, if it is not a vocational secret?"

"Oh, Francisco, you're here! Good morning. Excuse me, I didn't see you," replied Böhme. "I'm very glad to see you."

"Pleasure is mine. I haven't seen you for a long time. How are you?"

"I'm fine, thanks. Take a seat, please. Would you drink a cup of coffee?"

"Thank you, dear. Can I ask you what are you busy with?"

"Look at this," Böhme said and handed him the newspaper. "Again this topic—UFO." And he smiled. "You know my opinion, but read this text. My curiosity was attracted, and imperceptibly I became preoccupied with these funny calculations, which aren't any secret, of course. It became very interesting to me—unexpectedly even to myself—and I scribbled something."

While Francisco read the feature, the steward served him a fragrant Brazilian coffee, milk, juice, and biscuits.

"Does anything there impress you?" the host asked.

"Nothing especially," his friend retorted after a while. "There have appeared in the press from time to time so many messages about UFOs that they aren't much of a sensation anymore."

"Sure, but look at this, the second case. Let's assume that Earth represents one coordinate system and the landed object another. You see that fifteen minutes in the one system are equal to five days in the other. The problem is, whose fifteen minutes are equal to five days?" Böhme said and smiled.

"If we assume, first," continued the scientist, "that fifteen minutes Earth time are equal to five days of another's time, then one second of Earth time would be equal to eight minutes of the other coordinate system. In other words, the time in it will run at an incredible rate in comparison with ours—one Earth minute will fit eight hours of the other time. One could really turn there into a very old man in a very short time. Now, if we try to calculate the object's maximum velocity during its motion, we'll get this:

$$v = c\sqrt{-230399}\ \text{km/sec!!!}$$

c—this is the velocity of light or, written in another way:

$$v \approx 480\ c.\ i \quad \text{km/sec}$$

where *i* is the imaginary unit.

"But such a velocity is just unthinkable. It is impossible in our world. Then? This result suggests to me that if we, all the same, assume this velocity to be real, we should then consider the object solely as a messenger of an imaginary matter's world."

"You mean maybe a type of so-called exotic matter?"

"Yes, I mean just that. Still, in 1957 the mathematician Hermann Bondi and, from a certain time on, the phenomenally brilliant Stephen Hawking also carried out research on the problem of imaginary matter. According to the hypothesis, the imaginary matter's objects would always travel faster than the speed of light, and that without infringing on the principles of the Theory of Relativity. Just like it is in our case, by the way. This is a mirrored world to ours in which all is converse, an anti-world in which all is turned inside-out from our reality.

This is a world-antipode of ours, in which the time is running in the opposite direction, every event follows an opposite course of causality—in case of a blow, the motion decelerates, and in case of meeting a barrier, it accelerates. So, if we guess that our fifteen minutes have been for them five days, this is an upsetting notion, because it is in fact the opposite—not acceleration for them in relation to us but, in reality, a retardation of the time for them."

"Our future for them is past and vice versa—our past for them is future?"

"Yes, this hypothesis, however, calls the Big Bang Theory into question. If the imaginary matter really exists, then the Universe's history would be completely different. But this issue, as much as it is interesting, is scantily studied. But in order for me not to run off just on that, let's consider the other possible case, too.

"Once the object has landed, its velocity is equal to zero, i.e., the times of both coordinate systems are equal—fifteen minutes. Consequently, from Einstein's first postulate for the soldiers beside the fire, fifteen minutes had passed, and fifteen minutes had passed for the spacecraft's crew, too. But for Valdes, de facto five days had flown out, if we assume his description as veracious. Still, no man's beard can grow for fifteen minutes as much as it normally would in five days!"

"So, the corporal had really aged ahead five days in only fifteen minutes!"

"Yes, and in such case it remains for us to assume that he was placed in some completely unknown, uncommon, in some alien, extreme conditions for him. Let's say he had been found in some isolated chamber which imitates the state of the bolide during motion, with the aim to retrace his body's reactions as well as his bearing in such conditions."

"Something like our space-training centers imitating the conditions of weightlessness which are characteristic of outer space?"

"Exactly! It's possible, for example, that Valdes had been put under the influence of a powerful electromagnetic or gravity field receiving, under the object's motion, an oversize sub-light velocity. And for this reason he could get partial amnesia—he lost his memory and does not remember anything that occurred to him inside the object. In that case, it becomes clear that one second aboard the spacecraft is equal to four-hundred-eighty seconds, i.e., eight minutes Earth time. If we go on further, it is seen that twenty Earth days represent only one hour of the time inside the spacecraft. One year of Earth time is equal to eighteen hours and twenty-two minutes, while ten years amount to only seven days and four hours. In other words, if we've had visitors, let's say, from the star Ross 154, they have hopped over to the sun for only a week, while on Earth, ten years have passed. ... It's stupefying, isn't it?"

"Yes, indeed. But, in such a case, what velocity have they scudded with?" Francisco asked, intrigued.

"It's just fantastic for our measures. It's got a maximum velocity of299,791.81 kilometers per second! An overwhelming velocity! Only six-hundred-fifty meters per second slower than the absolute one—the velocity of light. Can you imagine that?"

"I can't. Light can move only six-hundred-fifty meters from the front of this ship. No, no, I can't imagine!"

"Yes, only six-hundred-fifty meters faster before it. This for us is a fantasy. And it cannot be otherwise after our spacecraft move at the laughable velocity of twenty kilometers per second, while this craft's velocity in relation to the velocity of light is 0.9999978! The relation is this: twenty toward three-hundred-thousand kilometers per second. For the present, we can't even dream about reaching it!"

"And to understand how far away we are in our development from such a civilization that has maybe attained the acme of its perfection."

"Is it possible for us to convey some knowledge, some information which is of interest to these brothers of intelligence concerning ... whatever it may be? This is funny. Or, are we perhaps able to adopt something of theirs by which they would communicate with us?"

"In this sense, we're alone in the Universe, even though, at the same time, there is life teeming around—some much lower or much higher than ours, which determines the impossibility and needlessness of such a contact in a certain moment."

"In that case, when it exists, the contact is always unilateral—from the higher to the lower life. This being so, the latter cannot usually make sense of … cannot understand the existence of this contact. The reason is that they use other laws of nature which are still unknown, still not found by us. They can even gather crushing accelerations under which no one tellurian could live. Everyone would be torn to atoms far before their maximum magnitudes. How they decided what this point was, such that Valdes was left unharmed, I can't explain to myself."

"As they have decided all the rest of the points," added Francisco.

"Yes, it's so, given that they can traverse such vast space with such easiness. The utmost distant where they could arrive from by this maximum velocity describes the sphere's diameter of nine-hundred fifty-eight light years, i.e., this velocity allows them to be situated not more distant than nine-hundred fifty-eight light years from here. This result completely refutes Professor Bergman's allegation that, to a distance of three-hundred parsecs, i.e., of nine-hundred seventy-eight light years from us, there are no technical civilizations on our level or of a higher development. On the contrary, the difference between his prognosis and the result here is exactly twenty light years. They're so developed that they gad about the cosmos and roam quite easily within the boundaries of this space, normally and without exertion, in a sphere of nearly three hundred parsecs in diameter."

"All of this is so if these calculations were not guesswork but facts. Were they? I mean, if the case of the corporal is authentic. However, can anyone prove that?"

"Unfortunately, no one can. We can't trust reports of such meetings. Such contacts always arouse doubt about their veracity, but then, I regret to say, this is a reason for a full denial—too condescending and easy—by the serious scientists about the already mythical flying saucers. They'll let them seem like tall stories. Maybe in view of avoiding ridicule and loss of face."

"Well, yes, but in such a case, all the same, you couldn't really disprove Professor Bergman by this well built-up tower with a clay footing."

"Naturally, these curious calculations will remain only an entertaining play at my leisurely disposal here and now—an amusement instead of solving crossword puzzles. These reckonings are just small-mind exercises, sudden and pleasant as childish remembrances, but, I think, I won't forget this very interesting UFO case, which will certainly stick in my mind. After two weeks, however, I do have serious work ahead of me, my friend. Therefore, what I especially need right now is rest." concluded Böhme. "Let's go in," he suggested, and both of them were off to the fancy villa.

3

His eyes opened slowly, and then shut again. His consciousness was roiling. The thought, *I think ..., therefore I am*, passed slowly through his mind as the first reaction of coming back to awareness. *But ... where ... do I find ... myself? ... What ... has happened ... to me?* His brain overstrained itself to bursting coming out of the coma, out from the dark of unconsciousness beyond which there is nothing. His eyes roved about the room. It was a domed room with a pale-green background, and the air was slightly sweet with crimson roses. He lay motionless, chained to something stiff and unable to budge even an inch despite his will. Or, at least, he guessed so.

I ... am ... Paulo. ... Paulo Roberto. ... What ... am ... I doing ... here? The lad tried hard to remember how he had gotten into this sterilized igloo. Into his consciousness emerged, heavily and slowly, some dim, vague and as if quite remote reminiscence.

He had successfully taken his examinations in the university. He had had a day off and, together with his cousin Manuel, had gone angling in the river. So… Suddenly Manuel cried and pulled him by the hand. Not far from them, behind their backs, a huge mushroom had appeared. Or, to be more precise, it was not a mushroom but a completely spherical ball of dark-blue color. A knobby balloon shining with inky luminescent brilliance surrounded at the middle by a dark-red rim that didn't seem to be connected in any way to the sphere. It was about forty feet in diameter. So … At once, imperceptibly, no one knows how, they found themselves inside this luminous orb. They could still not collect their faculties when several medium-size figures came near and surrounded them. The figures were dressed in what appeared to be red, tight-fitting neoprene suits with none too big metal hoops glimmering on the chests from time to time.

They did not talk, either between themselves, or to the two men. They only indicated to the boys by their eyes what to do. In this unusual manner they ordered them where to take a seat. Paulo managed only to count them up—there were eight figures . One of them came stealthily near to both lads and gave them some green liquid to drink. And from this moment on, Paulo no longer remembered anything. Where was he now? And since when? How much time had he *slept*? And Manuel? Where was Manuel? Why was Paulo not seeing Manuel anywhere? What the hell did this hall represent? An operating room? It made his hair stand on end at that thought.

"Take it easy, Paulo, take it easy. Manuel is safe and sound and is at home. Don't worry about him. Nothing bad will befall you, either. This is not an operating room but your berth." Beside him he heard a mellow timbre and, raising his head slowly, Paulo saw one of the figures close to his feet. "Call me Speax. I think that we'll become friends."

"Friends?" Paulo's temper rose. "But who are you? Or, to be more precise, who are *you*? And by what means do you know what I thought just now? By what means do you know my name?" He shuddered with fear as he asked his questions.

"You'll learn, you'll learn all. Only have a little patience. I had to come to see your condition. You can already stand up and move freely. Now I'll leave you alone for a while. I'll be back soon."

Oh, my God, am I captive?, Paulo thought to himself. *Am I a young test beast in the hands of unknown ravishers, of space invaders? Impossible! Impossible! I'm imagining it. I'm suffering from hallucinations! It seems to me rather like a movie, a bad mix of images and not true at all. But, for God's sake, how can he know what I think? That's impossible. Surely I'm dreaming! That's impossible!*

Paulo looked at himself. He did not dream. His clothes were missing. He was also dressed in red, just like them, in some suit of easy-fitting, light and pleasing, soft stuff and with the same metal hoop on his chest. He wished to rid himself of these clothes and to look for his own.

Paulo began to take the upper part of his suit off. Suddenly, he felt strong shivers. He began to feel a keen, piercing, uncaused fear, an incomprehensible sense of trouble. Unexpectedly, his body wrinkled, while his eyes and head pained him so hard that he reeled. He began to go faint and to be feverish; he felt nauseated and dizziness in front of his eyes. He was covered in goose-flesh of pain, as if hundreds of thousands of small needles were run into all of his body with their keen steel tips; he stood electrified as if all his hairs stood on end from stored static electricity. Paulo did not understand whether this was real or only a false sensation, but as his first unthinking, subconscious reaction, as an instinct of self-preservation, he pulled the red kit back on. Right away he felt relief; he came around, calmed down, and regained his normal condition. Only then did he understand that these suits with their soft stuff were not the latest fashion fad and not uniforms either, but probably protective garments against the deadly intensity of the mighty electromagnetic field around him, which could shorten his life. The glossy metal hoop on the chest was maybe an anti-gravitational ring that neutralized the crushing artificial gravity in the spacecraft to the point of normalcy for them. No, the ring was not a mere adornment; it was a life-belt, not a foppish decoration.

The lad sat down on his bed and rested. He looked around himself. His eyes could not catch on many objects. The room, or, to be more precise, the chamber in which he was located was lit up by a slightly bright light that did not tire his eyes. The chamber was almost empty. Besides the bed, in his cabin there were several white, egg-like stools around a low cylindrical table. On one side of him was some strange device that he would not have perceived if it was not tinted in ochre and thus outlined against the general reseda background. A door, or at least some opening, was nowhere to be seen. It was as if he was located in a pressurized bell tent, a round cell wigwam of an ultra-modern penitentiary. The only diversity on the wall was a dozen parti-colored spots, probably sensor-buttons, situated over that ochre device. Obviously, they had some special function, jointly and singly, because they were in different geometric forms, too—triangles, squares, circles, and rhombs.

Paulo was just ending his brief view of the scanty furniture when unnoticeably, opposite him, a door glided noiselessly upwards from below. He had not even suspected its existence, since nothing betrayed nor suggested it—neither an aperture anywhere, nor even a fissure the size of a knife's tip. The door drew into the wall and then went back down. The berth took on again its monolithic appearance.

It was Speax. Right away Speax noticed the sick air of the crooked, in-slightly-grimace face of the boy and immediately understood all. Paulo was pale, faded, dull-eyed, and lightly bearded.

"You tried to take off your suit, did you?"

"Yes. I didn't know that it's dangerous."

"You shouldn't do that. In fact, the mistake is mine I should have warned you." This sounded like an apology by the Speax's mouth.

He was medium-size, slim and slender. He looked youthful by reason of his smooth face. All of this, together with his small nose and screwed-up, cold, grey eyes, made him a strange-looking representative of this alien race. He had tight lips drawn in at their ends. Besides that, Speax had a lengthened, but not round, face, without protruding cheek-bones; a face that did not change its serious, as if stony air. He had a keen, intent, and piercing gaze, even as a physical sensation; a gaze which penetrated into and through the person. Speax himself was impenetrable, but when he spoke, his features became as though softened. But, just then, something strange occurred—or at least it seemed so to Paulo. Speaking was as if extrinsic to Speax. Sometimes the words came as though out of him, like a silent film where there is no synchronized recorded sound and it does not fit the actual actors' acting or, to be more precise, like a TV set when the picture and sound in the talking person are not in synch. Sometimes the words, as if anticipating his mouth's opening, came faster than their pronouncing, as though delivered directly with his gaze. All of this was scaring poor Paulo. But was it only that?

"Paulo," Speax began after he came near to him, "you have no reason for fear. We mean no ill to you. You are a participant in our experiment. I say *participant*, but not test-mouse because, although you are engaged in the research, this trial doesn't threaten you in any way—neither your life nor your health. Our purpose is to scrutinize to what degree the human psyche of your current time's level is able to bear the extreme conditions of a cosmic march to—"

"But you didn't ask me! You didn't want my consent!" Paulo interrupted him suddenly. "You infringed upon my rights!"

"That's right. But it's the first condition of the test—the stress, the psychological shock inevitable under such a situation, which you have already survived successfully, as we had expected. Out of several people examined before you, only you showed the best initial makings of survivor in extreme unexpected situations along with high intelligence, and that's why we chose you. We decided that your cousin, Manuel, could not bear the test, and we left him on Earth."

"*You* decided! You attack me, abduct me, and finally wheedle me! Really? And besides, Speax, I'll tell you something. I'm guessing that you aren't addicted to speaking, Speax. You aren't used to speaking at all! And that's not to my fancy, and it even boggles me."

"Sure, from where we are, speech is long forgotten. It became extinct long ago. It simply no longer exists."

"You don't say? Well, where are you from? And how do you communicate then if you don't speak with each other?"

"All right." Having sensed the irony, Speax tried to form a smile and took a seat by Paulo on the bed. "We're inhabitants of the star Omeron, a star not so bright in your night sky, and which you know as star 61 by the Swan constellation. It lies remote from you at a distance of eleven-point-one light years. It's a binary star composed of two red dwarfs. And since we passed your current stage of development a long time ago and are now in respective cosmic maturity, we no longer need this stage of intercourse—speech—among individuals in our society. We dropped this lower form and extent of communication in society and, as such, replaced it with telepathy. The bio-electromagnetic transmission of information to a distance ousted the sound-based one. Thus, we've realized a direct exchange of thoughts among the people, and they're no longer able to hide behind silence or to speak insincerely."

"You know, I'm beginning to get interested,", Paulo replied curiously. "So, therefore, you know, at every certain moment what I think?"

"Sure."

"And, therefore, you know my name and that of my cousin, too?"

"Yes. It's not difficult to set in or haul out something from your memory. And not only your name, but anything else, as well."

"But, in such case I'm laid in a very unenviable—no, something more—in a quite defenseless position," Paulo protested.

"It's nothing like that. You'll also soon master our language as one of us, and you won't feel blue."

"But, Speax, as I see it, you can speak quite like a tellurian, too. And probably you can speak every language on Earth without problems, can't you?"

"Sure, it's the same thing as a speaking man like you, a man using the well-arranged speech for dealings with his likes, begins making sounds and whoops in order to be grasped by some monosyllabic primates, a monkey, for example, in order to chatter with it. Yes, I can speak, because it is necessary now, and when I do it, it's for your sake only in order to surmount the stress, the jitters and thus to be equal in our communication. But before long, you'll be convinced yourself that this is a useless effort. For you've maybe noticed that sometimes your thought slips out before you can vest it into words, that it flies away before you can utter it."

"Thank you for saying that we, the people from Earth, are playing the part of monkeys!" a piqued Paulo uttered.

"Sorry, but it simply is the correlation between the intellectual levels. I want you to get my meaning correctly."

"Well, for a particular individual I can accept as normal his telepathic potentialities, but for a whole society it seems to me rather fantastic."

"On the contrary, there's nothing unnatural about it. This is only a way of communication and is simply a result of the entire evolution of our civilization. It's a consequence of our all-around development, but it's not an empty end in itself. However, we'll talk about that some other time. Now I'll tell you only that telepathy, as well as speech, did not appear overnight. Telepathy, as well as speech, arose after a very prolonged transition period. It was gradual at first, with only particular individuals, whom you now refer to by the common names of faith-healers and clairvoyants. The first speaking people were also worthy to be called thus. But after three hundred more years on Earth, speech will die out as a lower and less effective degree of communication. As such, it will be ousted by telepathy. If you want, you can see for yourself when you return to your native planet at that time. You can join in an expedition to the star Antares, for example, and when you set foot on Earth again you won't recognize it. About three hundred fifty years will have elapsed, and you'll see a different world."

"Oh, no! Thanks for the offer, but for the time being I'll pass up that suggested route. This voyage is enough for me. I suppose you aren't a tourist agency having a promotional plan to Antares?"

"I'm not speaking of tourism, Paulo. We didn't take you as a tourist. But if you don't want … if after all that you'll see, you don't wish to go on with us, we'll return you to Earth forthwith. However, you'll see only the beginning, only the first steps of your brilliant future, but not this very future for which, maybe, afterwards you'll regret. It's not worth anything to us to return you right away, while for you these sixteen days' journey will be just a half-month recess."

"In eight days you traversed the distance of eleven-point-one light years?"

"Sure, but why? Are you astonished at that?"

"Really, I should begin to gradually get used to all the surprises and miracles. But I don't know whether I can?"

"Paulo, for the present, I think I'll leave you to rest. Too many impressions and experiences are coming at you all at once. I see that you're rather tired. We'll see each other again when you have had your sleep and muster your faculties."

"A rest? Here in this cellar? You're going to leave me again in this igloo? This is a trap, Speax. I can't budge anywhere! If a man stays here too long he could go mad as in an isolator, a lockup or hospital room. I feel stifled. I feel like a prisoner here, do you understand?"

"Don't worry, Paulo. Whatever conveniences you wish, you can have them just by touching a finger on this orange little square. If you want food and juices, touch the blue circlet. If you want to take an aerial or water shower, put a finger once or twice close to the green circlet. If you decide to open the door, just stand in front of it—it will open by itself. You needn't utter anything aloud to it or do anything else. It's enough for you to just think it. The artificial intellect watches for all. It receives and deciphers your thoughts, just like me, and it immediately responds in the adequate way—for instance, to open the door."

"But if it does not open it?"

"Then touch the red rhombus. But don't go out before I show you around the spacecraft and make you familiar with it—you'll lose your way."

"And would you explain to me what, in fact, this keyboard represents?" Paulo persisted in his curiosity.

"This is a control board for your whole cabin, which, in addition to being your living quarters, is also a self-contained space module. All cabins throughout the spacecraft are for one crew member each. They are, so to say, life-boats in an extreme emergency. Besides being under central subordination as cabins, they also have their own autonomous regime of steering as capsules. Of course, we have working modules for production activity, too, which are three times bigger and which we can use as life-saving pods, as well, but they are located in hangars.

While these are only for an exceptional case, as final variant and all crew members cannot in any way reach these hangars. If for some reasons the spacecraft is in danger of certain and inevitable destruction, then in a moment all capsules will be in a position to detonate from inside and scatter in all directions, like splinters, at an initial velocity of ten thousand miles per second. They're supplied with everything necessary—their own engines and enough reserves for three years. And if they are not found by then, the astronauts can hibernate and put themselves into suspended animation. For that purpose, this bed you're sitting on is used."

"Has it ever been necessary to take this extreme action?"

"We had only a single case with the first models of this spacecraft. But all about that some other time. Now I really must leave you to take a rest."

Speax turned around and was off to the door discernible only to him. Paulo noted in his mind its approximate position relative to the adjoining objects. Speax stood in front of the door, and it lifted noiselessly. He went out, and it fell back into place. Paulo was left alone.

He looked around himself. Naturally, the parti-colored desk attracted him. He touched his finger on the little orange square. Right away, on the opposite side of the wall, a dark space opened up, and from there a wide, round bed glided in, while the stiff plank-bed withdrew into its place. Paulo threw himself on the round bed, stretching out on his back with the greatest of pleasure. Then he turned over onto his stomach and gleefully began to *swim*. But suddenly he jumped to his feet and parked himself outside *the magic carpet* again. He was hungry. The young man pressed his forefinger to the blue circlet with the first thought that came into his head. Less than a minute later, from a small aperture to the left, two hotdogs and a big tumbler of orange juice appeared. Well, that's what they called a Pushkin's Golden Fish! At that, it would fulfill more than three wishes!

While having his lunch, Paulo groped by a glance all of his lodgings. Something seemed to be missing in the interior.

Oh, yes! The aesthetic decoration, of course—it wanted works of art, and this created a despondent, grey, sulky mood in him, underscored by monotony and depression. Paulo *ordered* and, before long, he obtained several pictures by Rubens, Rembrandt, and Renoir—perfect copies of color holography. It was impossible to distinguish them from their originals, even down to the minutest details of their orgy of color, even in all their peerless diversity of tones and undertones, of tints and shades, whose magic harmony is just what turned t—hem into masterpieces. Besides that, as a sheer terrestrial, Paulo found spots to put two sculptures, too, which were shaped from a material unknown to him: a bust of Bach and Demosthenes—in full height statue. Maybe accidentally, maybe deliberately, the sculptures were put there as iconic top-symbols of his civilization, a civilization of sound waves—one personified music, the other speech. Now his dwelling seemed not to be a cellar or an atomic bomb shelter, but rather it resembled a luxury suite in a modern hotel.

Paulo stared fixedly at a charming picture straight ahead. All the images were astonishingly thin, and on the oval wall they appeared almost like mural paintings, so the vault above him was easily able to become the Sistine Chapel. His connoisseur eyes were mighty attracted by the beauty facing him. Paulo's attention was entirely absorbed in a picture by Renoir—*Bather, sitting on a rock*—whether it was because of the auteur's artistry in the very painting itself or the grace of the nude body depicted on it, he did not understand. He went nearer to the picture and examined it from all sides still more intently as an *arbiter elegantiarum* and admired both the artistry and nudity, both the brush and shapes. She looked real, and actually there was something nacreous and glowing in her. *The simplest themes are the most long-lived, as the artist has often said, having in mind the woman, as well. Certainly, he's right*, thought the lad.

Bather, however, also suggestively provoked in him to have a bath. He decided to implement his intention, and, for this purpose, he looked for the green circlet. He touched it twice with his finger. As a result, from above right, similar to a big nylon dropper, a bluish gauzy-cylinder descended, which, in fact, was a fully automatic shower stall.

After Paulo took a shower, the bath-cylinder retracted back up as if there had been nothing there a little while ago. At last he tiredly flung himself onto the bed. And only then did he begin to clearly realize his situation. He began thoroughly to muse, and at last he fell prey to conflicting emotions, as if two men lived within him. The one could not yet become reconciled with the abduction, while the other took things as he found them. His two *selves* carried on an intriguing conversation with one another.

Good heavens, did I dream? What's happened to me? Did I ever imagine? Have I ever thought, even for a jiffy, that this could be done at all? I couldn't dream this up. This is not my reality. This is more than fiction. But where does the former end and where does the latter begin? Just maybe it really is necessary that they would want to determine that stress threshold, that psychological barrier corresponding to certain intellectual levels beyond those we already perceive, so that we can ***fluently*** ***<u>understand</u>*** *their messages and normally the world of their phenomena. Only then, but not before, can we realize a bilateral contact. So, for that reason, despite all their continual visits, they have never, until now, and won't ever again be in official touch with Earth's civilization. For that reason, effective communication of all mankind must be prepared, not just particular persons or states and scientific institutions.*

By the way, who's to say that they themselves are ready? On the contrary, they're the last. And the course of action that could be done, as we imagine, to put it mildly, is primitive and narrow-minded. It is naïve and funny to think that they have to register themselves in a passport office to establish their identity in someone's chancery, even if it's a presidential one, or in a customs office. What new can we say to them? What can we understand from them? Nothing! Only the stress, just the stress will be really unsound for us—maybe even fatal. That's why until now the people of Earth only observe various random phenomena, such as UFOs, without being able to understand their nature; probably in much the same manner as a Neanderthal man who suddenly meets a helicopter in front of his cave. He will observe its possessor, too, but he won't be able to realize ***what it is****! He will look but will not see.*

It seems, however, that one has to be confronted with the problem, as happened with me, in order to fathom all that. He really has to experience all the absurdity of the situation and only then can he comprehend it all. Man is made like that. These regular visits to Earth are simply exploratory programs probing for and studying the intellectual level of Earth society. They're working visits with scientific aims and nothing else.

Well, for that purpose, I'm an excerpt of representative research? Or a probing trial? Why me, why must I alone be the rite animal? Am I the scapegoat?

All right, all right, but then why can't you accept the idea that you're an ambassador extraordinaire of planet Earth with an exceptional mission? Why can't you adopt yourself as a momentous mediator between two civilizations? Take your juncture here as a rare chance dreamed by each tellurian, as a matter of honor!

His eyes were slowly closing, weighed down by fatigue. The young man gradually dissolved in a sweet trance. The sleep was overpowering him, and because of that, he did not notice that, along with his eyelids falling and the gradual roiling of his consciousness, the light was gradually dimming by itself, until at last it became thoroughly extinct by the time Paulo fell asleep. Obviously, the light was self-regulating, depending on the waking state of the occupant's consciousness. Along with sinking into the infinite abysses, into the depths of Morpheus's possession, a full darkness fell upon the cabin.

4

"Oh, you want to be closer to Earth, do you?" Speax was surprised at the changed furnishings in the cloister of his pupil, who was just ending his snack.

"Sure, you might say that," Paulo replied. "In order to feel comfortably himself, man always wants to create his own cozy nook, a snug spot where he will feel well—at least the earth man does." He took a sip of juice.

"I think we can proceed with our conversation, Paulo. You wanted to see and learn what is beyond this door, didn't you?" Speax said, pointing a finger to the wall where nothing showed the presence of a door. "Come and acquaint yourself with the craft."

They went out and passed a number of corridors, curved and spacious and were lit up by a dove-blue light showering from some unknown source but pouring uniformly everywhere. The corridors were wide enough for several people to walk past each other easily. Paulo jutted up a half-head taller among his well-meant captors.

The two men came into the enormous sky-blue round hall, about a hundred yards in diameter. Its cupola rose probably a hundred feet in height. To the right of the place where they entered was a huge screen which visually conveyed the craft's motion towards its destination. In fact, Paulo could not discern anything from the cosmos on this screen, because it seemed like a strange, black, round lens through which ran lightning luminous dots and dashes. Under this sub-light velocity, inspiring him with mysticism, all events in front of the craft were perceived inside it as images seen through a fish eye. No starry sky could be seen, still less could one delight in it. Various astronauts shuttled continually to and fro in the hall carrying out some tasks, obviously bearing on their duty.

"Paulo, this is the central control panel which, as usual, is on automatic control. Actually, until now it had never been imperative to proceed to manual control. One might say we're only passengers who can take the helm only as a last resort. The whole craft represents one constitution in whose brain center we're located."

He motioned around the room, to the screen, and to the crew.

"Maybe that's the reason why, from the moment I first got here, I've been feeling a strange sensation that this space liner has some organic origin. It's far from any idea I've ever had of a spacecraft—no steel or metal in its construction."

"Well, it's not of organic origin. This craft is an artificial intelligence that is akin to the biologically one in its functions and properties. It incessantly watches the changing environment outside and automatically keeps the normal for us inside. *Daring*, as we call it, is just one of us. Come, I'll show you something."

They set off toward the opposite side, and when they were about thirty feet away from the wall, they stopped. Then Speax harshly screwed up his, by nature, narrow eyes and concentrated for a second, staring sharply at the wall, as if he wanted to burn it to ashes just by a look. In a jiffy, a piece of it suddenly changed its color from blue to grey and transformed at once into a luminous screen.

"Look. This is the cargo section with the launch capsules I told you about," said Speax.

Paulo saw approximately twenty dark-violet spheres, each with a rusty-red ring around its middle. He had once seen a sample under other circumstances!

"These are cargo vehicles designed for industrial extraction of various rare chemical elements. We also use them during exploration of certain stars' planetary systems. They develop at the same speed as this craft does, but they have much less range—up to four or five of your light years."

While Speax was explaining, Paulo was curiously watching the screen. These violet globes, however, not radiating now light from inside, looked not ink-blue but rather darker—in blue passing to black, as well as the ring—dirty-red shading into brown.

"*Daring* has five big holds. Each has two cargo section-hangars like the one you saw just now. In other words, in each hold there are forty modules, and together they total two hundred. As you know, one module is served by eight persons, and you understand that the full crew is one thousand and six hundred persons," Speax added.

"Oh, but this is a fleet! Have you used them for research work only? Have you never used them with military aims?"

"If someone shows enmity to us, they could be used as military units, as well. For this reason, those bright round tiles resembling mica, are situated everywhere in order to deflect the mighty shafts of light beams directed at us from both natural cosmic sources and by enemies' surprise attacks. Until now, however, it has not been necessary to beat off attacks of space fusillades as a result of aggression. Among the stars, there are no robbers. Among the stars, there are no wars."

At this instant, three figures came closer to them. They were not tall of stature and appeared as weak men. It looked as if Paulo would not see any stout or tall people here. It was vague whether they were all such as these, but these three persons, like Speax, seemed even-tempered and self-reliant although they were young. Or at least they suggested such a notion of youths who don't grow old.

"Speax, is this our new friend?" asked one of them.

Paulo wondered why this one spoke aloud, but understood that he was the reason again—he, the tellurian man.

"Yes, please come meet him," replied his patron.

"I'm called Khoren, and these are Pat and Mot."

"My name's Paulo. You certainly already know that. I'm here on your orders." Paulo was incensed with a little touch of unexpected malice, even for him. Obviously, he had not accepted the facts in full, although he considered that he had. In fact, this had been a rather spontaneous outburst of indistinct feelings that showed themselves in this manner, and he did not want that. He realized his fault, but it was too late.

"Well, well. That's not the way to speak, boy. There're no orders among us. Nobody commands anybody. Speax, explain it to him. You'll take a fancy to us, Paulo, you'll see."

"I hope so, because what choice do I have?"

"All right, all right, we'll see you again. We're going to the central information hall. We expect to see you there."

Speax took Paulo in front of the command desk, which was located just beneath the screen. It was two billiard tables in size, and Paulo felt himself outside of it, like a child who doesn't know how to read but has opened a primer with pictures and is interested only in the pictures. After that, he saw where Speax's cabin was situated and understood where he could nicely spend his time. There were various playgrounds where he could go for sports, as well as a few smaller cabins where he could check his mental capacities through numerous logic games. In general, Speax showed him around all the halls and rooms of the craft that could be of interest to him. At last, passing again through a labyrinth of corridors, the two arrived at *Daring*'s central information hall. They entered.

The hall had the form of an old oven, i.e., a truncated circle base having a diameter of about two hundred-fifty feet and a dome about fifty feet high. It was an amphitheater filled with a great number of comfortable chairs raked upward for optimum viewing. The only straight wall, located just opposite the entrance where they had come in, looked like an imposing cinema screen. Probably important meetings with particular significance for all the crew were held here. On Earth, it would be a congressional hall for seminars, conferences, and other such meetings. There were resolutions proposed and taken here. In fact, this was the library, the memory of the craft—all the information of their own star and neighboring stars' history up to three hundred parsecs away, along with a detailed stellar catalog of the whole Universe, were concentrated here. In case of need, each armchair could, by remote control, switch on or off a part or the whole of the holographic image across the way.

Khoren and his two friends were already there. Paulo and Speax went nearer and sat down beside them. The extraterrestrials threw glances at each other and understood one another in a twinkling.

"Well, Paulo, now you'll learn things that no tellurian knows," Speax began. "We'll reveal to you some of the secrets which agitate so many of your minds—from the child to the old man. You, as a man from Earth, may have noticed that all great events on Earth submit to a precisely determined, cyclic recurrence. The natural calamities and cataclysms—floods, conflagrations, record-breaking temperatures, earthquakes, volcanic activity, diseases, epidemics, etc.—intensify and mark their peaks every eleven years. And this is the solar activity cycle. All the epidemics, from the plague of the seventeenth century in England to AIDS—the plague of the twentieth century—coincide with peaks of heightened solar activity."

"Besides that, however," Mot parenthesized, "the activity intensifies in society too. Have you ever paid attention to the fact that social calamities also are the strongest every eleven years?"

"Have you noticed that the most considerable wars and revolutions all have occurred during solar activity's maximum?" Pat added. "Not to say anything about the Great Revolutions. Clearly there exists a connection between them, their exact conformity with a natural law, a mutual agreement."

"I don't understand what you're talking about."

"All right," Khoren picked up, "you know that the Great English Revolution began in 1640, the Great French and American Revolutions burst out in 1788-89, and the Great October Revolution of Russia was carried out in 1917. At the end of 2023 there will break out still one more Great revolution as a result of the deepest, the most exhausting world economic and energy crisis leading to a new world war."

Mot thoughtful said slowly, "The nationalism, racism and the Islamic fanaticism, especially as worked out and directed by a handful of satanic minds of the new *globalism* doctrine, will unleash before that quite "unexpectedly" a new global war which will begin from the powder keg of the world—the *hottest* geographic region covering the lands from the Balkans to the Persian Gulf. That's why the revolution of 2023 will lay the beginning of the end of an iniquitous and ingrained with violence world."

Pat continued Mot's thought. "The third millennium's beginning, as marked by the Christian era, will start with the last Great Revolution, which will lay the beginning of the end of all evil. This event is irreversible. It's unavoidable, and there is no inhabitant on Earth, there is no power on Earth that can stop it or prevent it. This is the Second Coming of Christ."

"If we now juxtapose the years of all these revolutions," Speax began to expose the first secret, "you'll be convinced that they submit to an exact mathematical conformity with a law that affects your evolution and which determines the inevitability of the last Great Revolution. So, between the first and the second one there are one-hundred-forty-nine years, between the second and the third there are one-hundred-twenty-eight, and between the third and the fourth one-hundred-six years. Does that make any impression on you?"

"No, still nothing," answered Paulo.

"Look at this then: 149 is equal to 13 x 11 + 6, 128 is 11 x 11 + 7, and 106 is 9 x 11 + 7. You see that it forms a descending sequence by consecutive odd numbers—13, 11, and 9—complete cycles of the solar activity, plus always a constant of a half cycle by six or seven years. Why this is so I'll explain to you maybe later, since now I want to call your attention to something else.

"The events on Earth concern the big multitude's behavior on one hand, as well as the contributions of particular persons—talents and geniuses—on the other. One of the milestones in a society is the peak achievements of those particular individuals, of those great minds in various areas of science, culture, art, and politics, which leave a deep mark in society's memory."

"These achievements also submit to solar activity's cyclic recurrence," Mot added again. "In other words, the genius's muse, who exercises an enormous influence on society's life, also vibrates the most vigorously at that time. Perhaps you've noticed that in the works of a number of great scientists like Newton,

Leibniz, Huygens, Lomonosov, Coulomb, Faraday, Maxwell, and others, there exists an exact conformity with the law of discoveries following at an average of eleven-point-one years."

Speax continued the common exposition. "The fundamental theories and discoveries of Einstein also always coincide with the years of top solar activity. All geniuses are subject to the influences of this activity—Mozart, Bach, Verdi, Tolstoy, Dostoevsky, Voltaire, Rousseau, Kant, Hegel, Pushkin, Darwin … there's no need to count off all of them. So, ultimately, the matter reduces to the gist of solar activity—its causes and manifestation. And you certainly know something about that."

"About the spots on the Sun?" the earth man asked, perplexed.

"That's right. Probably you have asked, at least asked yourself, why the spots start appearing from a fixed latitude on the sun's surface. Why they move. Why their average cyclic recurrence is precisely eleven-point-one years, but not another. Why the spots change their polarity," Khoren joined in again.

"I've read some about all of this, but no one, until now, could explain in a satisfactory way the nature of all of these strange phenomena. There're all kinds of hypotheses, but they don't clear everything up," Paulo replied confidently.

"Well, you probably know that the main cause for the activities of the cosmic bodies is magnetism," Speax took up. "And that the bodies possessing mightier magnetic fields can influence the smaller or weaker magnetic field's bodies through their radial lines of force. Thus, on the Sun as well, as an object under certain conditions, it is possible at precisely stated intervals that a much stronger magnetic field can generate wells of activity, which you see as spots on its surface. Our binary star is old, and that's why it is almost exhausted, but we've made an artificial black body as an unseen energy source."

"Are you saying, by any chance, that you provoke the Sun's agitation by directing magnetic force lines to it?" Paulo asked, still more perplexed.

"That's right. Our sun, in relation to yours, is sort of like an entangled couple. And they mutually influence each other," agreed Speax.

“Really? But … but … how does that occur?” Paulo felt in a maze.

“I’ll tell you,” the cosmic man went on with his lecture, as a holographic scheme appeared. “Since the Sun, as every other star, has a strictly fixed slope of its spinning axis, at first the magnetic force lines that come from our Sun to it arouse small, local magnetic fields up in its highest latitudes. They show themselves as none too appreciable disturbances. Because of the Sun’s motion, however, in the course of time the magnetic force lines begin to go more and more down, in the same way the Sun’s rays descend more and more down from the pole to the equator of Earth under the changing of the seasons—as it does from spring’s coming to autumn’s beginning in the northern hemisphere, for example. Besides that, at every twirl around the axis, at every turnover of the Sun, the force lines bore increasingly deeper into its atmosphere—first the corona, and then gradually both the chromosphere and photosphere. In this way, ‘acne’ spots arise on its face, which are left there as ‘special peculiarities’.”

“In that moment when the force lines of the Sun and the ones sent by our star merge,” Khoren added, “when they coincide, it puts out a weak, primary ejection on its surface. The Sun’s rotation itself, however, makes this connection very unstable, quite brittle, and shakes it so that, at last, the respective line of force is inevitably wrecked, is ‘broken.’ At that very moment, the real ejection occurs that is seen from the outside.”

Highly impressed, Paulo followed everything in minute detail on the holography, as in an instructional film.

“Yes, I see. But now it dawns on me that back on Earth I had read a similar hypothesis somewhere. But those authors pointed out Sirius and Proxima Centauri, not 61 Cygni,” the student ejaculated.

Pat joined in the lively conversation. “The delusion is only in this. All the rest, that’s to say, the mechanism of operation, is just like that. Sirius can’t do that. It’s a dead star. I want to say that not only is there no developed reasoning life there, but also there’s no life at all in any form there.”

"In spite of all that, it had its civilization," Mot came forward. "But Sirius is a triple star, and for that reason it is very unstable. Less than two thousand of your years ago, Sirius B exploded as a 'semi-Supernova', as some of you call it, and transformed from a red giant into a white dwarf. We understood that from our observations beforehand, but, unfortunately, with a certain delay. That's why we couldn't prevent the explosion, but we could localize it. The risk existed, of course, and it was certainly not inoffensive."

"But the pledge was bigger than death—at stake was life!" chimed in Pat anew. "Not so much our life, we could easy dodge the catastrophe, but yours—of our inheritors by Gaya, as we call your Alpha Centauri, the Sun and mostly Sirius itself. That's why, before Sirius B began exploding, we carried out a life-saving operation on a large scale. We sent space emergency teams there, whereupon we had to extinguish the conflagration so that it couldn't spread and devour everything we had created."

"Good Heavens! That means we actually owe it to you that Sirius B did not burst as a normal Supernova, doesn't it?" Paulo asked, more and more dumbfounded.

"How can you account otherwise for how a star could burst as a *semi*-Supernova? How was it able its annihilating detonation to be localized on its own?" Speax replied with his own questions. "This could occur only under controlled intervention from the outside, since there's no such natural cause that can stop, or at least cushion, the annihilating detonation of a Supernova whose element sweeps away any manifestation of life around it. There's no such natural cause which, after everything else, could filtrate the aftereffects of such a global catastrophe."

"All this life-saving drive," Pat intruded upon the conversation once more, "was necessary, as Mot already explained you, to prevent the emergence from our clones, for a brief time, higher organic forms of reason on Gaya, Sun, and Sirius. Anticipating the forthcoming cataclysm on Sirius, we had to settle its civilization in suitable living conditions, which the Sun and Gaya offered. We had to throw to Earth that small group of people from the Bandiagara Escarpment in Africa. This is the tribe of Dogons, as you know it. Therefore, until now, the Dogons knew in minute detail all about the star Sirius, which you and all of your academic science still only guess at. They knew that Sirius and the Sun were *brothers* and show it in their queer rituals that recreate the relationship. By the way, thus did the myth of Nommo, their Noah and his ark, grow up amongst them as a story preserving their knowledge of actual events."

"But in that case, how then did the same myth arise in our history, too, moreover at a much earlier time, even though we didn't have the same doom as the Dogons?" the prying boy wanted to know.

Speax began his new expose. "The catastrophe in your case was not so powerful, but it claimed many more victims. An exceptionally massive asteroid, a piece of rock the size of a small planet, collided with such a mighty shock on Earth that its axis declined and displaced its orbit. Two big continents and a multitude of islands sank into the ocean. For that reason, we had to put into geostationary orbit those things that we could salvage until living conditions returned to normal. The Great Deluge, however, stayed in the consciousness of your ancient people as an indelible remembrance, as the most terrible event in their history."

Having seen the incessantly changing images of this awesome spectacle opposite him, Paulo let his tongue run away, turning to his alien mentors. "I wonder whether to believe my eyes? I can't perceive all of this as a reality. I remember, however, how Pascal had always been looking for proofs of the God's existence. Now they're in front of me—*you!* You're the embodiment itself of the God! You're the gods yourselves! While we thought that we were masters of our deeds on our own, that we developed in a natural way, according to the laws of nature –"

"But taken as a whole, this is so," Khoren countered, opposed to their apotheosis. "You—your Earth society—developed in a completely natural way just like inside a pregnant woman. The baby develops in the mother's womb quite independently and naturally, according to the laws of nature, and also out of touch with others in its own world, a world sunk in darkness and blindness. Does anybody meddle when it develops normally? No. All runs according to an initially instructed program which leads to the childbirth after a fixed period of time. You also are such a *baby* with an impending birth soon. Nature repeats itself again and again to a higher degree."

"You mean that just like an embryo's development, the evolution of our society subordinates to the natural laws but, all the same, it originates in a conceived cell?" Paulo did not stop questioning.

"As concerns the nascency of life, in general, on your planet," Speax continued, "this is quite clearly pointed out in one of the most ancient of your sacred books—the Bible. The creation of the world lurks truly in a clod of clay. One might say that, in the final analysis, man actually was created out of mud. For life was created by the combination of clay and water. This material turned out to be the most suitable for the origin of genetic code, since in Earth's conditions, only on the clay in a natural way may go off into simultaneous synthesis of peptides and oligonucleotides, and namely the water is that single and universal physiological dissolvent necessary for a carbon-based life. So, water was especially created just for this purpose—in the name of the life!"

"Although, as a chemical compound, it is rather unusual and even enigmatic, as well as illogical for your properties, because, under these temperature conditions on Earth, as a hydride of the oxygen, it should not be a liquid but a gas, right?" Pat looked at Paulo with an inscrutable smile as he expressed his ideas. "But you see, thanks to the water three and half billion years ago on the clay of your sunny planet, the first microorganisms emerged. And after that, the natural selection, through genetics and mutations, led to growing each branch and embranchment of the evolutionary tree's crown and to all vegetable and animal species on Earth."

"And, thus, until that fateful day when Man emerged—first erect, and then rational," Mot said, taking the floor again. "But for that purpose, it was necessary to apply precisely fixed doses of irradiation to create particular mutations in the monkey, which could transmute it into a man. Large groups, large herds, could be transmuted from monkeys to men, not one by one, not each individual separately, but only jointly, through a fixed number of consecutive mutations."

"This could occur through rising radiation from a repeated change of Earth's magnetic poles, with the purpose of briefly increasing the physical characteristics of these mammals—an increase of the stature for the sake of bigger muscular strength, as well as the skull for the sake of bigger brain capacity," Khoren added.

"The change at Earth's poles and the top increased solar activity assume the role of catalyst of enzymes, which harshly, and at a leap, repeatedly intensify the flow rate of the chemical reaction, i.e., the social phenomenon or the scientific discovery. For example, the solar activity catalyst selectively determines certain reactions in the social retort at a place and time; it incites both the masses to social conflicts and strictly determinate persons to strictly determinate creative work—just as the enzyme contributes to strictly determinate substances to enter strictly determinate reactions," Speax stated, ending the common lecture. But it was as if something was left half-expressed, uncompleted. Really, the studying would have to be continued on the next day.

Paulo was sitting stunned from so much information that had been presented in such an unaccustomed way in still a more unaccustomed place. He was tired and even slightly depressed. He was in need of rest in order to recover his strength. The youth went back to his room and lay back sweetly on the bed. His head felt heavy, and he fell immediately into a deep sleep.

5

The next day, Paulo's four tutors were waiting for him in a smaller, but more comfortable room resembling a study. The furniture everywhere was super modern. Speax was sitting behind a slim, gauzy, glasslike table on a chair made of the same matter. Straight ahead, Pat had ensconced himself on some strange dove-colored sofa, while Mot was sitting nearby on a chair molded to the shape of his body and drinking some beverage. Only Khoren stood upright and watched closely on a hologram the trajectories of various spacecraft flying in the deep cosmos.

Paulo looked round this new situation. Speax stood up from his place and stepped toward Paulo, asking, "How are you, my friend? Did you have a good rest?"

"I'm fine, thanks. I have been thinking over your words for a long time. The origins and development of our terrestrial life … and the whole of Earth's history … it's unbelievable. But really, according to the first records of our past, the first knowledge was given to Earth's people by the gods Anunnaki of Sumer. Are they, in fact, you?"

Speax began his account willingly, "Well, after the transmutation of the primates into men, they had to adapt to the environment. And once having taken on the contemporary human appearance, i.e., reaching maturity, their primitive society, just like a ripe ovum, had to be fertilized by the power, by the concept of State, through its material bearer—money. So, creation of the world can also be understood as conception of the world—yours—with the State, and the world with money, weapons, and religion."

At once Khoren joined in Speax's account. "For this purpose, the primitive men in different places on Earth had to be taught some basic knowledge and handicrafts. We had to teach them the first technologies, from production of pottery and glass to beer and sandals. We had to give them the wheel, chisel, and sword, as well as mathematics, writing, and, of course, the idea of God, of religion. You see how the first cognizant peoples emerged in Sumer, Egypt, and later in America, too? Peoples whose priests computed the astronomic time by their calendars no worse than the most perfect of your modern technical appliances. Peoples who suddenly and mysteriously appeared as well as disappeared from their native nests. 'Suddenly' and 'mysteriously,' they say now at your place, am I right?"

Khoren fell ambiguously silent, but Speax went on, "Actually, we had forwarded 'gods on a mission,' if I may use your words. I mean a working group that had to teach particular tribes the first lessons in a state system. And that meant that a class-structure of a society had to be built, one requiring it to have a hierarchical government in function, along with integrated urban planning—territorial, architectural, and communal. By rationalizing the concept of *property*, through to its manifestation of *private* property, for the first time a clear awareness of *borders* was conceived of as well. On that basis, the first amassments of human crowds in one place for organized joint life formed the first cities, at the same time being states too. Private property is the image on whose analogy the State was built, like the family is for private property. As per the technical side, Pat, please, tell him more," Speax coaxed, handing off the torch.

"Of course, I'd love to." Pat took it up. "Well, Paulo, concerning the technical side of the State's origin, as Khoren already told you, it was necessary to teach your forefathers some crafts, knowledge, and habits. Thus, they *discovered* the wheel and the plough, as well as bronze, earthenware, and cuneiform script. They tamed many animals, amongst them cattle. They built the first palaces, temples, and tombs. All these social and technical achievements in your human society typically occurred abruptly and in a very short time. So, in final reckoning, there was that sharp, sudden revolutionary leap forward into your civilization's development just when that transition was being carried out from a primitive to an early class society, when it took a radical turn in society's mode of life under its molding into a State."

"That's why," Mot broke his silence, "the first citizens on Earth have recorded that the State power is 'fallen from above,' that royal power both before and after the Deluge 'have descended from the sky,' as that is documented by the Sumerians. As you know, your history begins in Sumer. Just there, between the rivers Tigris and Euphrates, everything arises, but nothing, not even the names of the two rivers and the Sumerian cities themselves, have Sumerian origin. For, in the beginning, before Sumer, there were a people described as 'covert in mysteries' that were of 'unknown origins'—the Bulgarians, as they're known by their most recent name. These people are the first people connected with us, the 'gods,' and their rulers bore our names. These people are the ancestors of all of your current civilization, a people with high culture and established traditions, who were hungrily taken up by all their successors—Sumerians, Akkadians, Babylonians, and the others after them. All archaic peoples with a cult of the Sun—the Egyptians, American Indians, Scythians, and Thracians—have akin, almost identical customs, morals, and cultural records, in spite of the enormous, insuperable distances between them at that time."

"So, the epoch of the State," Speax took up again, "the whole period of its existence is only a 'pregnancy' of the Earth bearing its fetus—the human society that will be born as an independent material unit after three centuries. You know that the last three months before the birth are the most important of the pregnancy, don't you? Let us assume that fifty-five hundred years—as the program, the 'term' of the State is—are equal to nine months, and the last eighteen hundred years before the 'birth' are the most important for the future of your civilization. That means that from the fall of the Western Roman Empire until now, with the beginning of feudalism from the fifth century on, it has begun shaping your society as a future social unit."

"But besides this direct mode, we're using another one, too—a remote mode of surveillance," Mot cut in, changing the conversation's direction. "We receive the information on a special ultrasonic device."

"But what does it mean?" the youth asked, bewildered as before.

"It means that in order to explore some remote planet," Mot replied, "we send light signals in regular series-quanta for exploration, for soundings of the natural conditions on Earth, of its underlying geo-physical factors influencing the life on it—climatic, atmospheric, tectonic, and others. We constantly radiate these light signals in batches. In the same mode as sending magnetic force lines from our star to the Sun, we send light signals from our planet to Earth. Once such a directed beam reaches Earth, it wraps the terrestrial globe from the pole to the equator and enlaces it in a spiral. After the beam circles around your planet repeatedly in the form of dense 'windings,' it returns back to us now filled with information. You quite recently discovered the midget model of the quantum generator, which you call a laser. So, with such a quantum generator, enormous by your notions—with dimensions of your Moon—we collect the information we need. It is much more convenient, quicker, and takes much less consumption."

"Wait, wait," Paulo broke him off. "Wait a minute. You want to tell me that you regularly send light signals to Earth by an enormous laser and not one of us has noticed them?"

Khoren stepped up to Paulo, smiling. Now the hologram had changed, illustrating his description.

"Although we send these signals regularly, you notice them rarely. Maybe, because the light is the most widespread, electro-magnetic phenomenon in nature, it is just difficult for you to distinguish that one with an artificial origin. It was only in 1882 that an astronomer, named Monder, may have been the only one to have noticed one of these regular signals. After a strong magnetic storm as a result of increased solar activity and the supervened northern lights, he registered the phenomenon as a greenish, luminous disc in the lower part of the sky, east-northeast of Greenwich, ascending in a straight line with the Sun, moon, and planets, but with the difference being that it moved thousands of times faster than they. According to him, the disc disappeared in the west and, a little in the south after less than two minutes of crossing the meridian, it had already acquired the form of an ellipse."

"By the way," Pat joined in, "this is the reason for the appearance of so many optic phenomena like this being perceived by people as flying saucers or UFOs, which they're not capable of distinguishing from the real ones. It's not an accident that their numbers increase abruptly and greatly during maximum solar activity, because we usually send these light signals to Earth in parallel with the magnetic force lines' molding to the Sun."

"The astronomer quite correctly stated that the torpedo-shaped spotlight he had seen was unlike any of the heavenly bodies known to him, but it rather resembled the beam of a searchlight touching a cloud and creeping along its surface. He was not far from the truth," Khoren ended his exposition.

The earth man watched all of it, quite speechless.

"The next signal," Pat continued, "eleven years and eight months later, on August 26, 1894, had also been noticed. But again it wasn't fathomed, although its direction had been caught precisely from our star. In the night sky, over the two brightest stars of Cassiopeia turned exactly to Omeron, i.e., the star 61 Cygni, a luminous white spot was observed that suddenly burst with a very strong brilliance and almost at once transformed into a bright luminous disc with a diameter three times bigger than that of Jupiter."

Being dumbfounded by the heavy lecture, after a certain awkward silence, Paulo uttered, "Well, are you aware of something wrong in our development up until now, some breach of the functions or something more serious?"

As a honest physician, Speax answered him, "Your development is quite normal, and we expect a healthy *baby to be born*. It was necessary only once to resort to the use of the quantum 'lancet' to forestall any eventual future suffocation of the yet-unborn organism. There was a special light beam hanging over Earth for ten minutes, which caused the deafening detonation over Siberia's taiga in 1908. We had wittingly chosen that place as the most suitable land for it—waste, deserted, and far away from any big centers of social life."

"Do you mean the Tunguska event, by any chance, the Tunguska miracle?"

"That's right."

"Good Heavens, was that really your affair, too?" ejaculated the terrestrial.

"Look, Paulo," Mot jumped in before Speax could reply, "the information we received in 1882 concerning Earth's state was rather disturbing, unpleasantly bothering. In the next year, 1883, it was expected that there would be an exceptionally mighty eruption of the Krakatau volcano in Indonesia, which could endanger, to some extent, the normal ecological conditions on Earth, negatively changing the direction of your natural environment. This eruption would have darkened and polluted the atmosphere with ash to a height of six to eight miles that, along with other misfortunes from the lava belched forth, would have caused considerable destruction of the ozone layer."

"Combined with the industrial human activity," Speax added, "which had begun a hundred years earlier by using coal and which would continue still for one hundred and fifty years by using petrol, this result would have led to a substantial Greenhouse effect. And all of this meant certain death for your mankind. That's why, after precise calculations of the trajectory, place, and power of the detonation, we decided to send one extraordinary beam, much more powerful and more concentrated than the regular ones we'd been sending for observation. The purpose was to redress the disturbing ecological balance through recovery of the ozone layer and purgation of the atmosphere from the ash of Krakatau and the soot of man. The means was a plasma shell with medial power."

"A plasma shell? And how did you make it?"

Mot stood up, left his drink on the table, and approached the hologram. "This very strong and compound beam was composed of wide sheaves of weaker beams which caused the *unaccountable* lighting in the sky a day or two before and after the detonation—these weaker beams anticipated and followed the central beam, the very one that caused the detonation itself. At its entry, while still on its first 'winding' around Earth near the North pole, the beam cut into the low layers of the atmosphere where its energy was delivered into the air. It was in this way that molten plasma was generated in the form of a super, massive-ball of lightning that blew up with a vigorous rumble. This event on Earth was observed as a fireball glowing white, which, at the moment of bursting, was seen as a slanting, luminous, white-shaft obliquely directed seventy to seventy-five degrees to the higher layers of the atmosphere, a shaft penetrating amid enormous slivers of yellow-brown clouds on the background of the fiery glow in the sky."

"It seemed like a light cone receding with its apex pointing to the high parts of the atmosphere, or, to be more precise, as a white-bluish pipe ascending its upper end in perspective amidst the clouds. Namely like a pipe, because, just in the epicenter of the explosion, all the trees survived untouched, while everywhere else they were brought down like sticks. The otherwise awesome pines were scorched and mowed down radially and evenly," Pat added finally.

"But I've always thought that this explosion was a catastrophe caused by a spacecraft with an atomic engine," the lad cried out. "Now I'm convinced that I was wrong because of this reason—the damages were insignificant, limited, and considered. The undamaged trees really show a fire that was stifled still at its ignition, something that is impossible with an atomic air explosion. Besides that, the radially situated splintered trees, as well as most of the undamaged ones in the epicenter, suggest quite unambiguously the explosion of an ionized pipe, of a hollow plasma flex, but not of a thick monolithic body inherent in every spacecraft," the student reasoned like a detective watching the living picture in front of him. "Only now do I understand why there's no crater in the taiga, nor any dangerous radiation, except a slight, trifling rise in the natural background radiation, and why there are no cosmic particles—not even a milligram of substance! In short, now I understand why there's not any material evidence there of some natural or artificial fireball." Paulo analyzed the event while all the time closely watching the grandiose spectacle on the hologram.

"But what normal man would have started to cross the cosmic ocean with so primitive and dangerous engine as an atomic one? This is sheer suicide. Only a romanticist sucker doomed to death or a kamikaze would agree to do this. One more thing—if you had some quicker wits, if you had noticed the direction of the slope, the angle of incidence of the 'meteorite' as per the felled trees, you would have to guess that the signal came from us and nowhere else," Khoren said, ending all discussion.

6

The picture was unutterably grandiose and obsessing. Amongst the all-absorbing dark, amongst the dense black infinity of the cosmic wilderness, emerged a reality which surpassed even the maddest dreams, even the most distempered hallucinations. Along a hundred million miles, stretched an immensely enormous cluster made from strange technical installations; they were connected so that they formed a colossal, spatially folded, linear polypeptide chain. Obviously, at first sight the perceived disorder in the whole of this construction was only ostensible, while in fact it seemed this construction submitted to a strict order and regularity. It was impossible to distinguish which were natural and which were artificial planets and satellites, all they connected with in between were countless tunnels. Maybe all of them had an artificial pattern. These probably were plants, laboratories, and cities in apocalyptic dimensions, which formed a mass of cosmic agglomerations like nerve ganglions—everywhere big, medium, and small glittering nacreous spheres; big, medium, and small shining orbs, large cosmic pearls amongst the ocean of ebony insensibility.

But there was still something impressive in the entirety of this magnificence and greatness. This was the star. It was a binary one. The two blood-red suns illuminated with a slight crimson fire at the closest part of the whole 'polypeptide chain,' and lots of the nacreous pearls had scarlet gleams. Their total mass was almost equal to that of the Sun, but they were only half of its size. This was a rather older star compound of two almost identical red dwarfs circling one around the other. Obviously, the light and the heat of the star no longer served its civilization. As it became clear later, the energy sources of this civilization were various artificial, autonomous suns, used according to various industrial and everyday necessities.

The gigantic spacecraft was slowly moving nearer a branching of the chain at its end and was looking for a wharf to lay alongside. The craft was built from four imposing spheres that were connected to form a tetrahedron with stout, gigantic, cylindrical tunnels that were bluish and short. It looked like a colossal carbon atom that had emerged from the dark as a majestic symbol of organic life. This craft, as well as its space capsules represented thinking organisms with artificial super intellect and perfect nervous systems, which worked in full coordination and synchronization with the higher human beings that ruled them.

The landing-place was probably dozens of thousands of miles long and about half that wide. It looked like a laminated iron on a cosmic scale and was corrugated in a number of places and connected from below, with some sectors of the first station, through long, rounded, thick-walled tunnels or corridors. This was a construction of flattened-out, parallel corrugated sheets with countless canals scattered on them, like pores connecting the complex with the undermost station. Thus, from these corrugations multitudes of stories were formed, obviously for landing different kinds and classes of spacecraft with different dimensions. The biggest ones landed on the uppermost story, while the smaller landed on the lower, covered by the super-structural sheets.

In the receiving-passing terminus, Speax and Paulo entered a double concaved discoid capsule, which, obviously under a strong pressure in the environment, swept with unbelievable velocity along the huge tunnel. All people and cargo were carried in this way. In the eyes of the terrestrial, this resembled blood's movement in an artery. This capsule was just an erythrocyte resembling it, not only with its form but also with its red color.

They travelled so for about four or five minutes. Under this impetuous velocity, they probably had passed a rather great distance—whether ten, fifteen, or twenty millions of miles, Paulo did not know and could not know. Everywhere around them flew countless such red discs. Some other transparent "bubbles," many times bigger, were carrying something that looked like military equipment, and there were various cigar-shaped, elongated, or stellated flying objects. And probably every one exercised its function exactly. One could not help but be astounded by the impressive mathematical accuracy and precision of the whole organization of these apparent fabled beings. And it seems this was only the beginning.

As proof of these observations, at that moment something unexpected and awful happened. Paulo became a witness to an unprecedented cosmic catastrophe, which happened here only rarely—once in several dozen thousand years. About ten thousand miles from them, which meant close by, some huge fireball, some Leviathan piece of iron, just like a shell, cut with all its might into the otherwise stout bright tunnel with its thick walls. In a twinkling, from the inconceivably wide hole, an incalculable quantity of the vehicles broke forth like a geyser and all flew outwards into the cosmic space in one direction. And then Paulo was left still more highly astonished at the perfect organization that dominated everything here. Those transparent "bubbles," scary with their large size, were, at that moment, immediate witnesses of the catastrophe and abruptly picked up their speed beyond recognition and rushed after the stranger. Obviously, these battle aircraft were defenders of the system. They pursued it, and in a very short time caught the fireball that had been led astray by gravity. Though it was dozens of times bigger than they were, they encircled it all around and, by directing a series of strong shafts of light, they evaporated it.

At the same time, enormous quantities of the carried substances welled up, as blood would from a wound, and flowed in an imposing spout out into space. But here also the rescue operation was just beginning. Without panic and continually passing their way, various cigar-shaped flying vehicles were directed to the improbably wide opening. Their numbers continued to increase. These spindle-shaped capsules began to stop up the bore's throttle by clotting with each other in some queer way. In a short time, the opening lessened considerably, thereby tangibly lessening the outflowing stream. Before long, all was finished. The entire hole was closed, and all began to run normally. For the time being, the wall was still very thin and quite brittle. But a second jab was not expected—a second jab on the same place was only slightly probable. That is why in the disaster area just a few of the spindle-shaped capsules were left, while, at the same time, others thronged—star-shaped or hedgehog-like vehicles—which were obviously some engineering structural corps that had come to rebuild the inner layers of the wall that, until a little while ago, had been leaking.

All of this enacted drama was possible for Paulo to see, owing to the quick wit of Speax, who reacted to the danger with the speed of lightning. He had reversed the engine with a jerk and in this way had managed to considerably slacken the pace of their capsule. After neutralizing still the drifting capsule, Speax cold-bloodedly pulled a short but tricky maneuver and, through repeated intensification of the magnetic field, managed to adhere the capsule to the tunnel's wall only a mere thousand miles from the ominous breach so that the craft was not able to be carried away by the common stream of other, countless capsules flowing out into space. This was the first fact that made Paulo think that all these capsules flying by them did not contain intelligence in themselves. The only capsule that evinced intelligence was rescued. It was theirs. That is why all other capsules which submitted themselves to destruction under the breach's occlusion showed no acts of heroism and self-sacrifice as rational beings, but were fulfilling preliminarily determined operations as robots. They were programmed to do that. They had to act precisely and only in this way in extreme situations like this.

"Can it be true that all these fighters flying over are not ruled by men even when it has to do a complicated and multi-directional rescue like this?" Paulo inquired, perplexed.

"No, they're bio-automats, just an ordinary means of production, which are programmed in an appropriate way, having a designed behavior beforehand, as per the concrete situation. Men have much more important tasks than plugging up chest embrasures," Speax explained.

The journey went on for a few more minutes. As they raced at breakneck speed, passing along dozens of offsets and curves to the left, to the right, up and down, the space around them shrank more and more, and the tunnels' light dimmed. These trunk roads increasingly narrowed in diameter, from a span of two hundred miles, they diminished to just two miles. It seems these capillaries meant the coming of some outskirts. As their speed tangibly decreased, in front of them from below, a deep cone cropped up and, just like in a whirlpool, a part of the stream traveling before them plunged into it. They followed it. In a twinkling after that, behind them a canal-lock shut, pressurizing the drum in which they fell. This was a rotary roller or something like a centrifuge that turned around its axis. Paulo could not get his breath. From this headlong rotation and descent, he felt faint, and his head began to buzz. It was good that it didn't take long.

After making a half turnover, the *centrifuge* stopped, the canal-lock opened again, and the cone, this time with its base downwards, emptied its load, which also included the capsule containing Paulo and Speax. It was quite obvious that it was a transition from one space into another, carrying a substance from the former to the latter, where the *centrifuge* precisely represented exactly the effect needed for that particular carrier type. The carried substance, for a split second, was discerned by the carrier's built-in artificial intelligence, and only then was it allowed in any further. The carrier, relieved of the burden on the other side of the border layer, turned back again to its initial position. So that casual, noxious, or alien visitors could not penetrate the place, they would not be allowed very far inside the Promised Land.

And it really was the Land of God.

The two travelers found themselves as if in some other dimension, or, at least, it seemed so to Paulo. Everything there looked unreal to him, as in a dream, trance, or fairytale. It already went beyond, not only the scope of all kinds of human notions, but also all that had been seen up to now, however grandiose it was. In front of their eyes, in all its glory and might, it opened out to an awe-inspiring sight.

There was a planet-brain. It had an almost ideally spherical form with a diameter of about one million miles. But it was static, i.e., it moved neither along an orbit nor around its axis! This was an artificially-created planet protected by a dense envelope against its surroundings. It ruled over and was served by this entire complex constructed system, which was spread out for a hundred million miles in space, and connected as a whole.

Even the highest skyscrapers on Earth looked like nondescript dots visible only under a microscope in comparison with these that were here. Towering at a height of seven hundred miles, densely arranged one next to another, girdling all the planet, were hyperbolically concave sideways, funnel-shaped, mighty craters on circular bases bearing in upon themselves—every one of them—and mighty spheres, as well, with diameters between three hundred and fifteen hundred miles. They fit tightly together on the surface.

But the mind-distracting giga- and tera-polis constructions were the hanging cities. They were scattered in the air up and down at different heights—between a thousand and ten thousand miles, compound pyramidal constructions, like Eiffel Towers magnified dozens and hundreds of thousands of times, but with different numbers of elongated growths coming out from their tops ranging from three or four to several dozens. These were monolithic tetrahedrons, and drawn in at their ends were long, thin *threads* that seemed hooked to an unknown place, someplace far away in the void where some of them were connected. Hundreds of thousands of floors shined on their surface like dots, red on the grounded globes and neon-bluish on the airy towers. Dozens of millions of people lived and worked inside each city.

The capsule with the two pilots was lightly lowering down.

"This is our planet, Paulo."

The youth was staring outside as though bewitched. He managed to utter with difficulty, "It scares me and captivates me at the same time. I've never dreamt of anything like this."

"Maybe because you haven't seen such cities-*glial cells*, to use neuro-terminology, situated so densely together. But we're a hundred billion inhabitants of this planet!"

"Aren't you cramped for space?"

"Nothing like that. There's enough living space for everyone. You'll see."

Their capsule orientated to one of the nearby pyramidal cities *oligodendrocytes* with four *growths* fading into the distance. After a while, they approached one of the middle floors and, after finding an empty landing-place, the flying disc touched quietly to its surface. The two men went into to a considerably smaller *centrifuge*, which only by Speax's orders admitted the alien Paulo into the interior of the habitat.

The host offered the tellurian an apartment the size of a basketball pitch.

"Here you are, Paulo. This is your dwelling. You already know what to do if you wish for anything. I'll see you again."

"Thank you, Speax. I really need some time to get acclimatized. I'm still giddy."

"I'll leave you. Take a rest."

"So long."

After so many exhausting adventures, the tellurian had to be left alone in order to come to his senses. Here again, he furnished his spacious lodging to his liking by using the sensor remote-control panel, which was the same here as in the previous spacecraft.

As a real Fate's elect, Paulo would see and learn so many secrets concealed and inaccessible to the earth man. What was still to come for him to experience?

7

Paulo fell fast asleep for many hours. He woke up rested and hungry. The lad went to the bathroom to have a wash. On coming back, he wished to have breakfast. After touching the blue spot with his finger, Paulo mentally asked for warm milk with honey and ham pasties. After no more than a minute or two, the order was implemented. The food came through an opening from the right and fell on a tray—things that earlier had not been there. Once the desired breakfast was delivered, the opening along with the tray disappeared again as if it had not existed just a second earlier. The victuals were packed in gauzy, nylon-like envelopes, yet they were not nylon. Paulo tore them open warily. The milk and the pasties were warm—obviously fresh. They were delicious. The pasties were crisp and melted in his mouth, while the milk just added to the zest. He asked for more. Already at a distance, the youth indicated the blue spot with a thought and ordered the same things again. He was deeply impressed by the fact that here, as well as in the spacecraft, he could have whatever he wanted without payment; he could get what he desired without giving coins or a credit card. This was very nice, by jingo! This was alluring, but quite demoralizing! It had been so already for quite a while, and not only here. Nowhere had Paulo seen either a shop or a trade center with commodities offered for sale, and no firms' advertising lights either.

While still astonished, Paulo saw his four new friends beside him. He didn't notice when and how they had entered. His guests watched him closely.

"Oh, you're here?" he said. "I don't even understand when and how you came in! Hello! Everything here in your place is so unexpected and unexplainable," the terrestrial stated, impressed.

"Hello, Paulo," his four friends replied.

"Speax, would you explain to me how this is possible? I see that it's the same everywhere. How, damn it, is this free-of-charge system constructed?" began the youth, astonished for the serial time by his free breakfast. "With us on the Earth, it would destroy the whole of social life. It would lead to general anarchy, to a disastrous chaos and breakup of all structures and relations in the society. It would, thereby, lead to its full stultification."

"You're astonished at the fact that you don't pay for the things you use? We've simply no money."

"But … but how is that possible? How do you make it? How do you sell it if you don't buy it? And why do you produce it if you don't sell it? This is quite unusual for me, do you understand? Explain this to me, please. All my other impressions in your technical sorceries pale before this enigma. Yes, namely, it's an enigma!"

"I understand you, Paulo," Speax replied. "You've lived in another world where all is for sale—even the body, even the thought. And herein lays the unhappiness of such a world. But, in its locality at this time, it's just not able to be otherwise. Well, I'll take you everywhere around all our plants and laboratories. I'll show you the whole production and consumption, and you'll see for yourself how everything is done and how it can be so. Along with this, I'll tell you how we've come so far, how we've achieved all of this—the whole of this society's organization. We have a disparate mode of production and, therefore, a disparate mode of living from yours. Because of that, we've acquired even the appearance of another living form—more sophisticated and more highly organized."

The five pilots started off again in their discoid capsule to some way still unknown to Paulo. This time they passed through tunnels with strange chinks, which closed with a jerk behind them like valves. All along the way, the tunnels were strewn in sections with these chinks, which opened up from the front and closed behind the capsule automatically, under the influence of strategically fixed light-impulses radiated by it.

"We no longer live on our native planet, Paulo," Speax proceeded. "We broke our umbilical cord with it a long time ago—it remained lifeless and deserted. But such is the fate of each placenta. As you already saw, we've built quite a complete, out-of-planetary organism with its own energy sources-suns. We used the planets of our star only for solid support while we built this living cosmic organism. They will be left here to their own resources in their eternal running until their own end, when we'll already be far away amid the space's abysses, traveling in the cosmic infinity like a huge cloud of organized matter, like a floating intelligence, like a self-dependent form of life."

"Yes, just like a cloud," Mot continued Speax's explanation. "We're scudding amidst the cosmos like a black cloud, like dark matter, and in the whole universe this is namely the prevalent form of the matter—ninety-five percent of its total mass-energy content, which, according to you, is missing."

"We, in a body," Speax went on, "represent quite a new social unit—an aggregate cosmic human, in whom you and I are only cells in the body, a *Homo Cosmicus*, whose activity is to 'sow' the cosmos with intelligence. The Logos pervading the Universe—that is all!"

Since they had long ago gone into outer space, the impression from these words was sharply deepened and became still more convincing with the visual picture of the system fading into the clammy darkness. Looking at this unusual form of life and higher organization of the matter, which spread in front of him and filled out the whole of his gaze, Paulo thoughtfully answered, "Now I already know what this dark mass round the 61 Cygni star is, between eight and sixteen times heavier than the mass of Jupiter."

Everywhere around them, crossing spacecraft, large and small, were coming, mooring, or leaving according to their function. Speax set a course for their capsule.

"Did you pay ever attention to the strangeness and the monstrous energy of the quasars?" Pat asked Paulo.

"I know only that they're young star clusters."

"Yes, they're *clusters,*" Speax began, "because they're hundreds and thousands of civilizations like ours piled together for a common industrial activity, and they're young, only several million Earth years in age, because they've only been connected only for a short time. But yet, in order to develop the mentality up to this degree, it takes much time, you know that! They simply can't be dated from billions of years. It takes time in order to evolve to this level."

"This monstrous power of every quasar," Khoren instantly backed up Speax, "is due only to the united resources of the society of civilizations it represents. That is why the quasars have super intensive and exceptionally concentrated radio waves spread such that it seems to be only an artificial radio source; for example, on a micro scale Earth is doing that only quite recently. That's why quasars are the heaviest masses in the Universe with a negligible-for-them point volume. For the compactness, i.e., the concentration of mass, is the common quality of each society, from the human brain to the quasar—maximum density in minimum volume."

"The intelligence develops in a stepped up and spiral way," Pat joined in. "The human brain has a hundred billion neurons. The next level is the civilization of one star, as we are, representing a social brain by a hundred billion men. The next stage in the spiral is the society of the civilizations in one galaxy acting as a galactic brain with a hundred billion civilizations, whose first activities are the quasars. Do you think their location is accidental—out of the galaxies? On the contrary, in order not to foul up the environment, their industrial activity is always carried out away from built-up areas, far from any busy centers."

"The last level, known to us at least," Mot intervened, wanting to give his share in this new discussion, "is a society of civilizations that include all galaxies as a Universal intelligence by a hundred billion galaxies. Now, you maybe understand on which stage your Earth society is situated. Only when it obtains the right to life, i.e., only when it is *born,* after it takes the first steps of an infant child, and long after its initial spelling of our alphabet in order to learn its mind, only then can it take its own road. But for all of this, there will be the necessity of one hundred thousand Earth years. And then, before you set out on the wide road of the cosmos, maybe you won't forget to leave a sign of affection and gratitude on the planet-mother, as that was done by the first sun civilization a billion years ago."

"Was there ever another civilization on Earth before us? A billion years ago?" ejaculated Paulo.

"Not on Earth, on Mars. There's a monumental sculpture which reminds us of it. Here, look." Speax fixed his eyes on the hologram, but it was clear; there was no picture in it. "Evidently there's no information about it in this module's storage. We'll have to wait for a while until it can be sent by central storage. But you won't be bored."

Slowing down their speed, the five navigators now came close to a dark planet circling in orbit at about five-hundred million miles from the star. Its surface could not be illumined by the red dwarfs because of the enormous remoteness from them and the small intensity of its light. This planet had a very complicated orbit trajectory because of the perturbations caused by the two separate stars' gravitational masses, as well as by the social system located near them. The capsule turned into a whirled flight around the planet and established stationary orbit.

"Here is the quantum generator by which we regularly send light signals to observe the planets of closer cosmos, including Earth. It always operates in auto mode. I mean, it operates regardless of whether we're here or not, and it runs flawlessly. You're lucky. Look," Speax said, pointing a finger straight ahead.

Precisely at that moment, and lasting for about a minute, a powerful shaft of light erupted like a protuberance from an enormous crater towering at a height of about a hundred miles from the surface of the planet and directed towards Earth.

"In twenty-two of your years," Speax continued his lesson, "when this shaft comes back, it will be reflected in one of those mirrors and will be received at the information center down there, which is located precisely in the focus where signals arrive, not only from Earth."

The planet's surface and structure was striking. One could see "rivers" at the foot of the awesome "volcano," whose deltas flowed wide. They could be likened also to strong interwoven roots around the trunk of a mighty oak tree. There were "plateaus" and "mountains" built out of complex engineering structures passing under and over each other. They were all built of very rare chemical elements, which were very scarce on Earth. Plasma flowed in the "rivers," and the "mountain" ranges were covered with "forests" by densely set metal ribs. The sight was icy and dull. They had nothing more to do there. Therefore they started back, very carefully passing through the system of mirrors surrounding the planet.

The space module shot out into space.

Paulo stared at the black sky—there was no familiar constellation. There wasn't that beloved arch of heaven with its invariable, "immobile" stars. The Sun was probably thereabouts, far away. He tried to find it in this chaos of stars.

Suddenly the hologram appeared. The information they wanted had arrived—a satellite photo of Mars. The young man saw two amazing megalith buildings on the planet's surface. One of them was a pyramid, whose Atlas stature soared defiantly at a height of nearly five thousand feet, i.e., it was ten times bigger than the Great Pyramid in Giza! Not far from it, however, was something still more impressive—the relief effigy of a woman's face, a fine oval with pleasant features, clearly cut, spreading across an area of several square miles. The well-defined outlines of a woman's head created the illusion of a human photo. If one did not know this was cut out in the rocks, he could think this was a black-and-white photo of a living woman with profound and sad eyes, not rock buildings of overwhelming sizes on the surface of a dead planet. What building skills it must have taken to create this impression!

"This is an effigy of a young woman, chiseled like a death mask, which time cannot erase. It has remained intact to this day," Speax uttered. "The Martians had a taste for beauty, don't you agree?"

"Yes, undoubtedly," the lad replied, "but our space stations proved there's neither a highly developed nor any other form of life on Mars whatsoever. There's neither a civilization nor lower organisms."

"There isn't, but that doesn't mean there *wasn't*," Khoren joined in the conversation. "And, in fact, it's the first civilization on your star. Now Mars is really a desert, but once it was a double, a copy of what the Earth is now, a garden of paradise."

Mot continued Khoren's thought. "Now Mars is an abandoned placenta, like Earth will be in a billion years, too—lifeless and uninhabited. This process of the transformation of Eden into a desert, the transformation of Earth into Mars, has already begun. Look at the earth globe—this is clearly seen, especially north of the equator: the desert zone is already very wide and it includes the whole of northern Africa to eastern Asia as well as the western half of North America. In the south from the equator the process is running too—in South America, southern Africa, and almost the whole of Australia.

"So, in a billion years," added Pat, "Earth will be the same as Mars—a lifeless desert without forests, without water, and without a magnetic field. Right then, however, when Venus will bear its 'child,' i.e., its civilization, you'll have vacated your place under the Sun for it and will wander in the Universe in the form of dark matter. Your star has been awarded the rare chance of giving life to several generations of civilizations."

"Venus?" the youth asked, perplexed. "But one couldn't even think of life in the infernal conditions on that planet! Under those baking temperatures and crushing pressures, it would be impossible! This is absurd!"

"But you judge everything based on your measures, Paulo," Speax picked up again. "Why should life on Venus be carbon-based? Why should it resemble yours? Life can exist both at lower and higher temperatures compared to yours, and the respective forms of life are as normal as terrestrial ones are for you. Near Saturn, on its satellite Titan, for example, under a temperature two hundred degrees lower than your normal one, there exist chemical compounds synthesized by us, based on one of the salts of carbon and the ammonia as a solvent, which lead to the creation of primary bio-organisms. These compounds have properties very close to those of proteins."

"Titan's people, however, won't be titans at all," Pat added. "On the contrary, they'll be dwarfs compared to you, because they'll be very short—no taller than two-and-a-half feet and, in some cases, a little more than three feet. But this doesn't mean that these creatures, breathing methane and drinking ammonia, will be less intelligent or inferior to you."

"But to them, your terrestrial temperatures will be equivalent to scorching swelter," Khoren parenthesized, "unbearable heat, while on Venus these temperatures will mean a numbing cold."

"Venus is at the same stage of development—the end of 'protozoa,' as the Earth was a billion years ago," Pat chimed in again. "In other words, that great qualitative leap forward in the evolution connected with the emergence of eukaryotic cells and the beginning of their sexual reproduction has already been accomplished there."

"The obligatory conditions for the origin of life are several, and Venus also fits them: suitable mass of the planet, solid surface, comparatively constant and optimal radiation coming from its star as a result of an almost circular orbit, and especially the availability of a solvent of the physiological medium, which, for you, is water, but on Venus it is vitriol," Mot ended the group's exposition.

"What? What?" the young man stared.

"Yes," Speax continued, seeing Paulo's eyebrows rise in surprise and horror, "as a medium for intercellular interactions, vitriol is the most suitable when the base of the organized matter, the base of the living cell, is silicon. Silicon life is possible under your crushing pressures and unbearable temperatures, reaching a thousand degrees Celsius, as Venus's temperature is exactly normal for this kind of life at nearly five-hundred degrees Celsius. That is why on Venus there is now the same shaking volcanic and tectonic activity as there was on Earth once; the same mighty storms with thunders and whirling hurricanes with speeds up to two-hundred-twenty-five miles per second rave, together with extremely powerful electric discharges in the atmosphere and the initial ultraviolet radiation. The same dense veil, the same blanket of thick clouds creating, on the one hand, the same hothouse effect, which does not let the sun's rays get back up into the atmosphere and, on the other, the same abundant, ceaseless rains, only, instead of water, they consist of vitriol."

"In other words, the phenomena on Venus are the same, but, with respect to life, everything will be just the reverse of Earth's conditions—there the plants will inhale oxygen, and the humans carbon dioxide," Pat explained, smiling.

"So, in the stomach of a hungry Venusian working with a computer of diamond chips, i.e., on a carbon base, it is not hydrochloric acid that will be secreted to digest the food, but an alkaline liquid similar to water in composition, and the Venusian's ulcer will be something like common rust at your place," Khoren inserted wittily. "Of course, this is only one of our experiments aimed at creating another biological species, another human race, another form of life, but also known in the Universe as life based on the reverse, inorganic base. However, for them it's completely organic. If your chemistry means carbon and all the rest, then the Venusians' chemistry will be silicon and all the rest."

"I can hardly imagine myself going into the bathroom and having a bath in a tub of vitriol. You understand, don't you? The problem is who will turn the tap off afterwards," said Paulo sarcastically, looking at Speax.

"You're quite right," Speax imperturbably brushed off the attack. "The Venusians paradise of silicon is, in fact, a real hell for you—even more than a hell. But on Venus, everything is the reverse, as Pat already told you. Do you think it is mere accident that it turns around its axis in a reverse direction, and so slowly at that? Don't you admit that it may be due to the 'disturbing influence of some interstellar invader,' to quote the apt remark of one of your scientists?"

"What about the absence of a magnetic field?" Mot threw in.

"How can you explain the fact that the planet which is closest to Earth hardly ever experiences a tidal interaction with it?" Khoren added.

"But this isn't all," Speax continued again. "The nascence and development of life itself on Venus will take place in reverse order. What I mean is that it won't begin from below upwards, i.e., from water to land, like life on Earth, but from above downwards, i.e., from air to land. Its origin won't be the ocean, but the atmosphere."

"Simply because on Venus there aren't any oceans, and there never will be," Pat completed Speax's thought. "The reason is that if, like on Earth, a part of the atmosphere was condensed, that means the temperature and the pressure would drop to values comparable with Earth ones, and thus the silicon life would fail. You certainly know that if all the water in liquid and solid state were to be evaporated from all the seas and oceans on Earth, the atmospheric pressure would increase four hundred times?"

"If, however, this happens on Venus," Khoren interceded again, "if part of its atmosphere was condensed and, therefore, the temperature and pressure were decreased, then nothing would remain there except for seas and oceans of vitriol. There would be no life, either on a carbon or a silicon basis."

"So, after all, these infernal conditions for you," Speax picked up once again, "are necessary for life's appearance and evolution on Venus. Its atmosphere in the immediate vicinity of the planet's surface, its air as it touches the ground, turns into a hot fluid, into a peculiar boiling 'liquid' having a density of up to one-tenth the density of ordinary water, which is optimum for the development of one-celled organisms. This is, in fact, the 'ocean' of Venus."

"Besides that," Khoren joined in, "the availability of a constant temperature, i.e., an environment without sharp temperature changes, is of primary importance for the origin and maintenance of life. Such a constant temperature exists on Earth as well as on Venus—whatever happens, it is *always* very hot there. And the purpose of such a scorching and impenetrable, dense atmospheric environment is, besides all other purposes, to maintain the perfect sterilization, a sterilization which is much better than that achieved at the best of your scientific laboratories and hospitals, and which is particularly necessary and of exceptional importance for the life namely of silicon intelligence, since it destroys the microorganisms that are injurious to it."

While this scientific discussion on life continued, the five flyers unnoticeably passed the whole way back and found themselves again inside the space organism. They returned to the quay and left their Earth guest in his lodging. He had a new portion of information to think over.

Thus the time slipped by for Paulo. Day by day, step by step, he was initiated into the secrets of the Universe until reaching his early maturity.

8

After several minutes of wandering in the branching trunk-tunnels and after a breakneck rotation in a not-large *centrifuge,* their capsule entered a space full of huge, tall, narrow tanks and canals of grayish-white color, densely spotted by red dots, which were evidently some type of "pores," circular entrances. This was a very complicated labyrinth, composed of these tanks, which were confined by walls fifteen to twenty feet thick with cut-through canals and "vesicles" in different directions, having openings of one-hundred-fifty to two-hundred-fifty feet wide. This was a labyrinth, but not in a flat plain—it was three-dimensional. All this reminded Paulo very strongly of something similar. But what, what? …Oh, yes, of course. He had already seen this labyrinth in a biology book when he had been preparing for a difficult exam. This unsightly, architecturally ill-proportioned, and strange outfit resembled an ideal endoplasmic reticulum. It was connected with the boundary layer at its upper end. The lower end—the end that was right across from where they had come—was also connected with some other boundary layer, evidently separating it from another compartment.

"You see, my friend," Speax began, "we're in one of the numerous sorts of production units. This is an average plant, which doesn't differ much from other plants of its kind. We created such social production in these patterns, which are similar to the activity of the living human body. Each production unit, including this plant, represents a cell that is very close to the human one in its principle of functioning. Besides their specific functions and structures, all cells also have common ones. They are quite independently interconnected and carry out their business, i.e., their economic operations related to production, transport, and delivery by themselves, without human interference, but this business is as successful as that realized with human participation and even better. Everything is automated, not because it's an end in itself, but because it's metabolism. In other words, all the social production and reproduction is organized so that, without any human interference in it, an automatic economic interaction is effected between the different production units-cells, which are programmed for a strictly particular activity, just like a metabolism. There, above, the synthesis of proteins is accomplished and, as you see, the quantities are industrial. And since this process is particularly well developed, particularly intensive, the tanks are quite numerous and densely spaced. In other places they're not developed to such an extent."

"If you're interested in this," Pat went on, "later we'll show you other plants very similar to this one, which produce many other products. Let's go some further. Here all kinds of products are separated and prepared for transport for orders that have been received. The memory of this production unit, depending on the order, remotely sends a command to those orange bio-robots, who sort and prepare the products."

All this was done with such an astonishing, lightning speed and notable accuracy that Paulo was delighted by the perfect precision of all the organization that reigned here.

"From here, the products that have been prepared are passed to the adjacent compartment, which is, in fact, the forwarding office. Let's have a look there, too," proposed Mot.

There the situation was rather different. It was a whole receiving-delivering complex, which looked incomparably more complex than the recently seen workshops for immediate production, because it had intricate structures with net-, grain-, and bubble-like forms. There the production items were packed. The main part of the whole complex again was a set of flattened, smooth, grey-white tanks, slightly bulging in the middle, with an edge pointed to that boundary layer separating all these sectors from the building in which the "computer" hall, i.e., the plant's memory, was housed. On both sides of the complex were small, silvery spheres like balloons, which served as connection and passage to the production reticulum from which they had come. Large green tanks were seen from the concave side.

"You must have already noticed," Khoren entered the conversation, "that the whole complex consists of two types of formations. The first type are the tanks—the three, flattened, green tanks situated parallel to each other with a convex curve towards the brain center, together with the gray-white tanks enclosed by three-layer walls, fifteen- to twenty-feet thick. The clearance of the gray-white tanks is eighteen to twenty-seven feet, and the distance between them varies between fifteen and ninety feet. In periods of intense functioning, a great number of apertures appear on the surface of the tanks so that it becomes as though perforated. The other formations are those "bubbles," with a diameter of seventy-five to three hundred feet around the poles of the flattened tanks. They serve as passage chambers, as connecting elements. These chambers, as well as the perforated surface of the tanks, appear and increase considerably during the phase of reception of the products to be processed in the complex."

"However, it's no accident," Speax parenthesized, "that this complex is located nearest the brain-center of the plant. This branching, netlike structure must be under the direct control of the artificial intelligence, because the most complex cybernetic activity takes place here."

"Due to the extremely large variety of the products made and their users, respectively," continued Pat, "they're stored in a great number of places, so that reception and handling are direct, and this presumes the requirement for faultless control and monitoring."

"As you can see," Speax indicated with a glance, "at this very spot, the process of 'reckoning' between the producers-automata takes place. You had asked me about this. The whole social production is manufactured only to order, but not for market, which thus is fallen off as necessary. When an order is fulfilled—when the delivery of the ordered item is made—the client 'pays' the producer that has served him, not in money, but directly with the means of production the producer needs for his production. Each producer realizes his production with direct deliveries to his users, doing without any merchants' services, so that, in return, he himself also turns into a user, i.e., each producer is simultaneously a user of his user, and vice versa. Such is the complete economic cycle for all the cells, i.e., plants, and it is repeated continuously, just like in a living organism. It's simple, isn't it?"

Different vehicles continued to come and go in front of the student's eyes. And everything matched exactly as Speax explained. There, that light-yellow oval disc delivered some greenish load, and took a pale-blue one for its return. Everything took place rather quickly too, and efficiently. The whole activity resembled the work of bees, only without their apparent bustle. On the contrary, everything there was done strictly according to plan, quite pedantically.

"You can see for yourself," Paulo's guide continued, "that this economic mechanism makes money superfluous, because the products are made not to be exchanged, i.e., not as commodities. And it's namely the absence of commodities that stultifies the existence of money."

"Money is nothing else but that universal and unique commodity in which all other commodities are measured and exchanged, isn't it?" Pat noted this well-known fact.

"In this way, the whole process of purchase-sale, which is a real waste of time, drops off. But you probably know that, in society, each economy is reduced to saving time," Mot parenthesized. "You understand, don't you? It means that our system is economically much more effective than any money system, yours for example."

"So, there are two conditions for products not being commodities, and hence the absence of their intermediary—the money," Speax explained. "The first condition is that there should be no human labor put into them, that's to say, the whole social production and reproduction should be fulfilled without human participation. The second one is that the material values produced should not be intended for exchange. Only in this way can the commodity, and hence money, fall away as a necessary intermediary in the carrying out of the economic activity of social reproduction."

"But, to reach this stage of society's organization, people need first to reach a very high stage of technical and social development of this very economic system of money and commodity. Without such an evolution, all this is unthinkable and impossible," Khoren generalized.

"For this is such a high technological level of social production's development when the commodity exchange negates itself. Up to that stage, it should be continuously developing and improving, but not turning into a fetish," Pat pointed the general way.

"Precisely, this is baneful," the main tutor Speax warned. "If the exchange remains, if money continues to rule, though already transmuted in a consumers' society, this always leads to self-destruction. Remember, *always*! For together with the exchange, together with the money, the State with its destructive activity remains, too. The State is only a reflection of exchange, which has come to legalize it, it is its constant shadow. The State is the first derivative of money. But we'll talk about that some other time. Look there now—this is the plant's artificial brain."

Paulo's look fell on a rather large spheroid in blue passing into violet. It had a diameter of over fifteen hundred feet and was punched all over in hundreds of places. The apertures were evenly spaced, again similar to pores. They were presumably channels leading into the inside of the globe. The whole of this brain block was situated in the middle of the plant, taking up about one-fourth of its space. The light was somehow very strongly absorbed by it. There was something chilling in the silence surrounding this mind. The "pores" had a diameter of about twelve to fifteen feet and were located at a distance of about forty-five feet from each other. Paulo waited intensely for something to happen with them. But nothing did.

"The approach to the inside is absolutely forbidden. We can watch it from outside only, but we can't go in," Khoren explained.

"Oh, I'm not in a hurry to go there anyway," said their trained boy politely.

"I can only tell you," continued the Omeronean, "that inside this center are several smaller ones, strictly specialized in different activities and operations. Each cell, i.e., each production, scientific, or housing unit has its *electronic memory* like this one. *Electronic* is a rather ancient, obsolete term, because this artificial intelligence almost does not differ from the natural one. Besides that, each cell has its autonomous power-plant whose source of energy is the cold nuclear synthesis, and usually it isn't alone. Depending on the needs for energy, such power-plants can be from one to thirty in each unit-base. In some scientific and production laboratories, for example, there are between ten and fifteen. Only as a general power source for our whole system do we use the energy of the thermonuclear synthesis of our artificial star, and thanks to this energy we can move about the space. But, in my opinion, we should already be going back. What do you think?"

Paulo had nothing against that. He only managed to glance from a great distance at the several power-plants Khoren was talking about. They were shaped like beautiful whipping-tops, standing still, and bathed in white light. Meanwhile, the five passengers in the capsule smoothly landed on the platform of their floor in the city-cosmopolis.

9

This planet was so beautiful. It was a blue pearl, just like Earth, but maybe two times bigger. The space capsule, with only two pilots on board, cut through the sky and headed to a chosen place.

This was a notably picturesque spot. It was as if these two men were located in the Garden of Eden where all was verdant. Virgin nature was everywhere. The planet was rife with life; it seemed like a fairy-tale.

"What's this planet, Speax?" Paulo asked his fellow traveler.

"The Planet of Wisdom. It's a special planet," was Speax's answer.

"Planet of Wisdom? Why do you call it thus?"

"It's because this planet performs a special function for us."

"What do you mean? I haven't seen one human here."

"Exactly, we come here only in special cases, such as in the present case—you. We come here only when some chosen people have to be taught, have to be initiated into real wisdom."

The two men were moving slowly. Both were dressed in long clothes, which looked like monastic robes. In front of them a magnificent view opened out—a beautiful cove with fine white sand and an emerald-blue sea. The beach was littered with big and small rocks. From afar, the two talking men resembled Plato and his disciple walking along the beach and carrying on their new causerie. The disciple got ahead of the tutor with his next question.

"Speax, maybe now you'd give me some explanation about how you've achieved all of this, the way you've created all the harmony and perfection in your society. After all the things I've seen, I'm still at a loss as to what way you've followed, up to now. Your civilization is a grandiose symphony of Life!"

"This was a long and painful process, Paulo. Composing this symphony continued for five thousand of your years. I mean its practical establishment. But before that, during a rather stormy period, the preliminary design of this project was conceived."

The Omeronean stopped and squatted on a boulder; the terrestrial took a seat by him. Speax looked at the endless sea expanse for a while, and then went on with the story.

"Then, in the epoch of the State, our ancient philosophers were split up in three general schools, in three directions. The first one was of the so-called *moralists*, who insisted on getting acquainted with 'the thing in oneself' first, penetrating into one's own Ego, and then getting to know the world around him. But not everyone could, and even fewer wanted to get acquainted with oneself, let alone with others. Thus, only individual elects reached those moral heights, which were the eternal goal, the eternal call for the existence of mankind, and which, for most people, were eternally unattainable, like a radiant horizon. Only individual persons changed for the better, not the whole society. But they died too, and everything had to begin from the inception and be repeated incessantly during the next centuries."

"Why? Is it impossible to change the world if everyone changes himself?"

"No, it's impossible. Never. Each civilization's history substantiates that. The gravest mistake of all those otherwise great minds was that they assumed that the change of society towards universal prosperity could take place only by raising the individual, not the social consciousness, only by preaching moral categories. They're also necessary, of course, but, for a radical change of the *whole* society, the very way of life had to change, and the least effective means of doing this was to preach. Each religion tried to preach, but, alas, it was completely fruitless. The orders 'Don't steal,' 'Don't lie,' 'Don't kill' practically didn't change anyone. The religious charity and mercy towards relief for the poor could never solve, and did not ever solve, these basic problems of society. And the religion also cost money, at that.

"Yes, religion is the most slippery and nasty politics. I'm sure, because religion destroys the society with the name of God! Two thousand years of our history prove that."

"Well, well, you know so much about society," the philosopher said, smiling to his disciple.

"And what happened further with you?"

"The second direction was that of the *technocrats*. They assumed that society could prosper only via the technological revolution, which continuously increased the goods with its transforming achievements. But this is an illusion. The high-tech revolution can only facilitate man's labor and constantly raise the limit of poverty, but it can never eliminate it. The rich earned still more through it, much more than before. Charity was demagogy; it was an attempt to ease a guilty conscience and … taxes. The hard, strenuous years of the first industrial revolution negatively affected both rich and poor people very strongly. But later, the computer era, the time of robotics, managed to dull and mitigate their mutually rejecting social interests by means of this very abundance of goods, which the technological revolution was offering. It was just then that the statement was made from a high level that the social problems of the world had already been solved, that mankind was in its prime, that its Golden Age had come."

"Really? But I heard the same dithyrambs on Earth too, when I was there!"

"Of course, it's normal for your time," replied the sage, smiling again. "But this is self-delusion, or, more precisely, mass media's manipulation of society. Man can be very easily beguiled, just by satisfying some of his physiological needs. But man had no spiritual needs! And in this way, he left off being a man. Because he stopped living for others, he was interested only in himself. Egocentrism, indifference, coldness, the rising stupidity on a mass scale rushed everywhere with all their might, like leprosy. It wasn't moral standards, it wasn't philanthropic charity either that could bring about the general prosperity of the whole society, if they didn't enable *every* man to freely earn with his work enough so that he wouldn't be forced to sell himself to others or to steal. And this was the philosophy of the third direction—the *social* one."

"The social direction's philosophy? What does it profess?"

"This school of thought pointed out that the sources of all evils in society, in the final reckoning, can always be reduced to two—State and money. That is why these philosophers accepted that the social revolution was the only way to general prosperity. They thought that it was a revolution that could neutralize the common poisonous effect of the State and money. According to this school of thought, the standards of the moralists can be certainly realized in all of society by cleverly guiding the technocrats' technological revolution. This was the essential fact—for these philosophers, the social revolution was nothing but a controllable technological revolution. It was the philosophy that we all adopted."

"It sounds to me to be the most convincing thinking."

"Yes, but the trouble is that in society, the State is always adopted as an eternal institution, and money is looked on as an inevitable but necessary evil. It came to nobody's mind that people could live without either of them, that society can do without these 'genetic marks,' that it can function without money and without State. This thought was simply fantastic, as though filled with utopian dreams, and that is why it wasn't considered seriously."

Speax got up, and the two friends continued their walk along the beach.

"So, the solution was to abolish money and State. Abolish them by continuously improving their functions, by harnessing them into a new social system. But this could not be done in a day. In order to achieve to this moment, to this final result, it was necessary first to master the process of growth of value, that's to say, the process of increasing money as capital should become controllable, like thermonuclear synthesis, for example. The latter could not be mastered earlier than the former."

"And how did you achieve that?" asked Paulo. "That is the question. Just that it seems impossible to me!"

"How that was achieved?" replied the Omeronean. "We simply used the growth of the value in such a way that each citizen could freely progress through his labor. To master the value process meant introducing such a repeating automatic production cycle, which rejected the domination of man over man. A cycle in which man, while maximally using the fruit of technological revolution, could not be deprived by any participant in the same process, meaning a cycle, which would stop the self-increasing of money as *capital*."

"Wait, wait a minute!" the young man broke off the conversation again. "I don't understand anything again. It's somehow a complicated matter to me. Please, explain this to me simply. What do you mean 'self-increasing of money as *capital*'?"

Speax took a small tapering valve from the sand, began to write on it, and picked up again.

"Well, look now. If you spent an amount of, for example, one-hundred-thousand in your at-present worldwide currency of US dollars buying a diamond from a jeweler, you would use the money just as money, i.e., there is simply a change of property and nothing else. Money in this case mediates the briefest deal on change of property of a given commodity—against the money of one-hundred-thousand dollars, the property on the commodity of diamond, is transferred immediately and from a property of the jeweler it becomes your property. It's otherwise with capital. With the same amount of one-hundred-thousand dollars, you could buy some machines and three or four workers, which could produce, under your name, commodities that you could then market for one-hundred-ten-thousand dollars. You see, the amount of one-hundred-thousand dollars is self-increased to one-hundred-ten-thousand dollars, because the money is spent as capital, not just as money. Money in the new amount is already not just money. It is *increased* money, which makes it capital. And those three or four workers are namely the ones who convert the money into capital, because they've created value, which is more than their own value that you paid when you hired them. It seems as though money increases by itself.

Since this increase is reiterated, it represents a process. And just this 'magic' of transforming money into capital is termed 'value increasing process.' But since it's a spontaneous process, at a high technological degree of society's development, it becomes dangerous to it and could destroy it. For that reason, this process must be mastered. Capital is not only money. It's a social relationship between living people, although through inanimate commodities."

"What do you mean under mastery of the value increasing process?"

"This was such an economic mechanism, that, like an avalanche, it swept away the whole parasitic layer of direct and indirect supervisors. This was a mechanism that stopped the chaotic functioning of the value-based laws thus that they no longer created a blatant social dissociation into polarized property castes. This mechanism created an automatic economy where everyone enjoyed his or her free labor, because everyone lived only by his or her labor. The capital as social relationship ceased to exist. And this coincided with the period in which biotechnologies, computerization, and gene-engineering had already reached their individual summits, their primes. They had completed their last phase of scientific and practical metamorphosis and were, of necessity, merged into a whole as a real productive force. Thus, the automation in the production led to unmanned technologies, to relieving man from the production and the automation in the trade to buying only through orders at homes. The former eliminated the need for workers, the latter the need for shops."

At this moment, an animal bearing a resemblance to a hind cropped up from the woods on the left, and instead of getting scared, it stepped up to the strangers. When this grace came quite near, it looked at them with its big black eyes and shook its head up and down twice. Speax smiled at it, caressed it with his hand, and gazed deeply into its black eyes, as though saying something to it. The beautiful animal jumped for joy and dashed back into the woods. Paulo saw just then the full harmony of man with nature.

They both sat down on the beach. Paulo took a flat pebble and flung it at the smooth sea surface. The pebble jumped maybe a dozen times before it sank to the bottom. Paulo turned to his tutor.

"I see your perfection everywhere every minute, Speax. But I'm not sure that we could accomplish that … we, meaning Earth civilization. We kill not only ourselves, we kill our whole planet. I'm pessimistic we could ever reach your level of perfection."

"As I told you, the evil within each civilization comes in two sources: money and State," Speax picked up his story again. "In the meantime, while we were mastering this process—the value-increasing process—and money had lost its terrible force, parallel with this, we carried out another unceasing chain process of increasing society's prosperity, which was known by our philosophers in the good old times as the 'dying out of the State.' In fact, these two processes couldn't help but being linked, in other words, they're mutually penetrating. They were the two sides of a whole essence. Therefore, we had to appease the State together with money. The State is a synthesis of social injustice and violence, it is their concentrated expression," generalized Speax. "However, there comes such a moment in a society's development when society can shake off the State. But society is not able to emancipate itself from the State and, thereby, from violence and injustice, either earlier or later than at that particular moment. It's not able to do this earlier because it's not yet mature enough for that, there aren't the necessary prerequisites; and if the moment is missed, it already will be too late—because everyone's satisfied egoism will be lethal for all."

A pause ensued, in which Paulo tried to make sense of the discourse up until now. "Good, but the State builds up order and security in society. How could it be so pernicious? How can people move on without it?" the youth countered after a while.

"Of course, I don't maintain that the State hadn't its positive significance for society," replied Speax. "It emerged to develop this very society. It originated to hasten the development of productive forces of primitive society and to advance the consciousness of the savage. The State is the very 'pregnancy' that prepares society for new life in new conditions, not terrestrial, but cosmic. That's why, at a given stage of its evolution, however, it becomes superfluous, even pernicious; it turns into an anachronism, a remnant, which is the case with your society now. And why does it become pernicious? I'll tell you in a while," said the tutor and rose to his feet.

"Come on, let's go." The walk continued. "Well, 'dying out of the State' was a painful process. It was a difficult, but beneficial effect on the whole of society: self-repudiation of the State through the three institutions representing it—army, police, and governing. This was a purposeful policy pursued hard during some hundreds of years, but not a willful whim of some statesman or other who had decided to win political influence and cheap popularity. For this reason, the continuous reduction of military expenses brought about a dying out of the army, a farewell to arms forever, not an incessant demagogy of replacing the obsolete destruction weapons by new and modernized ones that are more terrible than their predecessors. In this way, we gradually began to eliminate the danger of the most brutal, the most savage manifestation of the State's violence—war. There will *always* be wars, as long as the State exists. They're simply inherent to it. The greatest utopia, an unrealistic and false hope, is a world without wars when it is clad in a State military coat. In such a world, peace is always cracked at some point. Sooner or later, but always!"

Just then a bower appeared in front of them. It was so nice and attractive amongst all of the luxuriant vegetation. A cascade was bewitchingly rippling nearby, squirrels jumped on the grass and trees. Some type of birds melodiously warbled. The two conversing men sat down on a wooden bench around a table in the middle of the bower, and the Omeronean wise man resumed the discussion.

"Except for the army, the same had to be done for the institution for internal violence—the police. We also subjected it to a systematic and lasting dying out. We gradually began to avoid and eliminate the manipulation of society's behavior, its modeling into an obedient and foolish appendix to the State. The excesses faded out. With the growing of social consciousness, the need for police decreased.

"With the dying out of the administration—and here I mean the elimination of clerk bureaucracy—the government of society gradually gave way to self-government. And this meant that society no longer had a hierarchical structure. It acquired a synodical nature. People decided for themselves all tasks, both locally and centrally, without the need of political parties and governing compulsion, which used to mastermind them from on high."

After a short rest, Speax picked up again. "People became really free instead of being suggested to this idea from everywhere. They were no longer persuaded to this idea from the platform of Power. For what do freedom and democracy stand for? They—freedom and democracy—always serve only one class, the rich class, when it is in power. This class persistently instills into the minds of millions of poor people the conviction that they're free. But, in fact, they've never been free under its power, simply because the State always represents a non-free society, no matter how much people cry for freedom. The realization of a freedom is established only inside the boundaries of a closed system, as the State is, only against the background of a non-free formation, only where there is no freedom. As long as there is a State, there can be no freedom; at least, not for all!"

"Your thoughts are very strange about such fundamental philosophical concepts as *freedom* and *democracy*. In our universities, we won't ever be taught such heresy," the student confessed, smiling. "No one professor on Earth could maintain that democracy is a relative concept!"

"Of course, but no one professor on Earth could tell me what we've outlived. No one your professor knows what we've attained," Speax replied, returning the smile. "Yes, in each class society, democracy is a relative concept. Your modern philosophers don't hold this concept, but the ancient and Renaissance ones were convinced of it.

"Democracy is an illusion, a mirage, the delusion of centuries. Why? The translation of the word *democracy* is 'power of the people.' And there's no such power! Power of the people over whom? Power of the whole people over themselves? Then this makes the existence of this very power senseless. Since its subjects always have to be a minimum of two—ruler and tributary. And if the people is the former subject, then who is the latter? Power was established and exists for one reason: so that there should not be any power of the people, but only power of a part of the people over another part. The reason for the State being a State is that it's not a democracy, not a people's power, not a power of the whole people. Power in itself excludes the domination of someone over himself. The State is a feast for some people, crumbs for others, but never for all! The State is always oppression, never a freedom! The State is always a dictatorship, never a democracy! The law in itself is already violent, a dictate. This is what at least scientists, if not all people, must understand. Yes, precisely scientists. Because they were always courted, bought, or tolerated in order to be servants of the State. And they were also cheated when it was necessary, for the same reason. In the final reckoning, however, their scientific fugues and technical toccatas served one, and only one, purpose—immortalizing the State. The scientist had to understand that his noblest impulses for the progress of mankind sank right off into classified folders with a serial cabalistic number—the first objective being his annihilation! And after he had understood this, he had to stop closing his eyes."

"And what have all of these politics resulted in? Were they successful?"

"The dying out of the State had a particularly vital effect on society—*all* its members developed according to their endowments and inclinations, and *all* had free access to the top science and culture, education and health services. The reason was that all non-production expenses, which had formerly been appropriated by the State, were now directed towards these areas. Gradually, with the dying out of the State, the courts ceased their functioning as part of bureaucracy and, along with them, the prisons also ceased to exist, which exhibited the fact that the State is a non-free society. That means that dirty business—politics, with its small-party squabbles, rows, and scuffles, which invariably accompany it—was also overcome during that time. Thus, along with the dying out of money covetousness, corruption and thefts gradually vanished, and, along with the dying out of the State, ambitious place-hunting, envy, and malice vanished as well. With the dying out of both simultaneously, we buried all kinds of crimes forever. And since then we, at last, stopped being tossed between Scylla and Charybdis, as you say. I mean between violence and injustice, in this instance."

"And you've begun to live your new social life? From that, originated your present social life, your perfection?"

"An ideal was attained. The dream became a reality. Idealism turned into realism. Replacing a free society with a democracy, passing from a classless society to a State, already contains in itself the need for the reverse transition—the passing from democracy to a free society, from the State to a united society. Now, we don't know what freedom and democracy mean, not because we're totally engrossed and absorbed by the State, but precisely because we're free of it. Now we don't know what robbery, murder, and violence against personality are, let alone crimes against mankind and wars. We know no hatred. We have no nations. We're all a united people, citizens of Omeron. So, all those social evils, which the moralists wanted to reject also but in a utopian way deposited as a memory, they remained only as a past … a remote past. We attained the material and cultural prosperity of the whole society, which the technocrats had wanted too, but in an illusory, unreal way."

"Speax," Paulo uttered after a while, "all I've heard and all I've seen in my sojourn here urges me to think that I'm dreaming. All of this is located in other dimensions … it seems so unreal …"

"I must warn you, however, that another way of development is also possible, and it doesn't bode such a positive future. It's a way that leads to nowhere, though only as an exception, of course."

"What do you mean?"

"I mean that the death of a civilization is inevitable if it doesn't succeed in parting with money and State in due time. There are such cases."

"Are there?"

"Yes, such a thing can happen if these two malignant tumors of society are not eliminated. But it seems to me that it's time to call it a day. I burdened you with enough information, and you have to rest. Do you want to continue our causerie tomorrow after you have enough sleep?"

"Yes, indeed. My head is already heavy with so many new things. ...Well, let's come back to this."

10

During the next few days, Paulo rested. He engaged in sports in the fitness hall; after that he took a good look at his residential section in the immense vertical city-megalopolis. He was already allowed to use his own little capsule, which helped him travel within the framework of the city. Paulo felt himself as one of them, as a particle of this society.

Today was a day appointed for the student's new engagement with his four tutors. All of them met in the same small and comfortable study.

"Hi, my friends. I'm so glad to see you again," the recruit greeted his fellows with a smile.

"We're all very glad to see you, too, young discoverer!" Khoren volunteered, smiling back.

"It's a pleasure for me to talk with you again," Mot added, being seated as before.

"How do you feel, Paulo?" asked Speax. "Did you have a good rest? Did you have your breakfast?"

"I hope you're okay," Pat greeted their Earth guest last.

"Yes, I'm fine. For a few days I slept the sleep of the just—deeply and quietly. And the breakfast this morning was thumping. I'm ready for our appointment.

"So, during the past few days, I've been thinking over all that Speax told me. All your path … a thorny path … but glorious. You inspire me to believe in our good future. But, Speax, we finished our discussion at a point about another way of development also being possible, a way of death of civilization. By the way, until I met you, I always thought this was the single path of our civilization—destruction, death, and extinction."

"Yes, the last time we talked we got to the point that another variant is possible, though as an exception," Speax began the new lecture. "For instance, a planet … let's call it X. The people of X's civilization had passed the stage of commodity production realized by the direct participation of man, but they hadn't renounced the commodity, that's to say, their money system. And this proved to be their tragedy. Because, although their whole production was automated and performed by cybernetic robots, and although they had a technologically and power-wise highly organized society, over-satisfied, and satiated by everything, they still hadn't outgrown money, they were still divided into rich and poor."

"Their God, no—Satan, was the Commodity. It was an idol, it was a Moloch!" Pat parenthesized.

"That is why at first they replaced the commodity money, mainly metal, after three thousand years of use," Khoren continued the theme. "Paper money appeared in its place, which, we must admit, functioned sufficiently well to service the circulation—until it became necessary to replace it too, when the whole public production all over the planet shoved the participation of man out of it."

"Then the energy-information money—*infeneric* money—was invented," Speax picked up again. "By using this money, the commodity no longer had a labor value, but it continued to possess an exchange value. The currency unit—one biterg—had ousted all previous currencies and had become the single world-currency unit. And then it very nearly set off an irreversible fluctuation disaster."

"In their striving for maximum profit," Mot said, taking up the baton, "a group of financial tycoons had succeeded, through a number of underhanded dealings and clever moves, to achieve the largest exchange blow of all times. The bargain was made for about five hundred billion bitergs. At that moment, these honorable gentlemen didn't differ at all in their gloat and satisfaction from a group of blood-stained savages tearing and dividing their loot among themselves in front of the cave."

"But this excess profit almost buried all of people, even its owners," Pat continued Mot's train of thought. "Due to their deliberate error in the information that was fed to the main servers' center of their planet, an enormous amount of energy was erroneously supplied to several sectors only, which were property of these very businessmen. Almost all other sectors all over the world were blocked; they stopped existing simply because they had no energy."

"At the same time, however," Khoren added, "several of their full sectors were overloaded much beyond their allowable capacities. An explosion from uncontrolled thermonuclear reaction could happen at any moment. The disaster was within a hair's breadth of doom. If the profit had been only ten million bitergs larger, meaning if it had been just a bit higher, this would surely have been the end. But everything passed by a miracle. It was simply *chance* that saved all of them. This would have meant a 'spontaneous abortion' for this not-yet-born civilization."

"This abortion did take place, however," Speax added, taking the lead again. "Because what happened in a political respect?

"An important political threshold was passed that froze until the moment the relations between the states, which were divided, mainly into two major blocks, and led them to a 'cold war.' It could annihilate the planet even earlier, because it was making that critical destructive withstanding, which is characteristic of a lower level of the State's development. In a moment, however, and quite unexpectedly for all, this repulsion was overcome, and a period of cooperation, of mutual attraction between the states began, as the strongest hope of saving, survival, and prosperity of the civilization. But this was a popular fallacy. For the rich states continued to rob the poor ones."

"But nobody paid attention to that fact any longer," Mot explained, coming forward. "People's consciousness and thoughts were directed only in strictly specified channels. Gradually, in the course of time, the political borders between the states were obliterated, thanks to the improvement of the system for overflowing capital from one sphere to another, from one state to another. With that end in view, some new, large-scale continental unions were created as a result of the continuing glossy pledge to the peoples for their bright and wealthy future. But this was by no means uniting the forces of mankind, as was pointed out, but merely globalism, which meant a merging of all states into one."

"The borders disappeared, they melted, but the goal was merging globally in order to form the only one world Empire," Speax stated with a touch of bitterness. "The State as a violent institution for social injustice remained and functioned flawlessly! The life of ten billion human beings depended on the whims of 0.00001 percent of the population—those hundred thousand rich rulers who had ostensibly been chosen by all common mortal people to govern them. Poor folk, they thought they had chosen 'their' president. In fact, he was chosen by others—those one hundred notables, masters of the world, whose puppet he was."

"The total manipulation of public opinion assumed its exquisite and supreme forms—perfect, refined, without edges and without corners," Pat parenthesized.

"Yes, it was a society under the faultless shaping of human behavior. Smooth. Ideal," Khoren added. "People were turned into brainless bio-robots."

"There were two ways to achieve this," Mot said. "Gene engineering created meek citizens and racial warriors always devoted to the State."

"Freedom was regulated through a correction of the gene as a 'hereditary disease'—this was actually though a prophylaxis against expected future anti-State activity," Khoren continued. "The discontent was simply preliminary excised by the genotype. Thus, it guaranteed that no protest reactions would occur in the future."

"However, there was also another way—computerization," sounded Speax's voice again. "People were no longer wheedled. No such crude practice existed. Changing the gene was a considerably more difficult and expensive way. But in return, a graft in the brain! The miniaturization of computers led to the creation of the 'brain pill'—a cheap computer biochip grafted into the brain quite painlessly. A great invention! You eat turnip, and in your mouth you taste roast lamb! Great! The problem of famine on the planet was solved! Let the poor eat turnips!"

"These at first harmless, innocent chips were created with a dietetic purpose for overweight people," Khoren continued Speax's train of thought. "One could chew tasteless, low-calorie food and feel as if he was eating meat, sweets, or chocolate, and thus lose weight. The illusion was maintained by this very biochip. It predisposed the eating man's consciousness to perceive the dinner, not as it existed on the plate, but as a meal he'd like to eat."

"However," Pat added, "the diet was extended to freedom, too—a person's thoughts were also subjected to a diet: a scanty, even a hunger diet. Chips were initially grafted into the heads of the suspicious people, strange persons, of those prone to disloyalty to the State."

"At first they were transplanted only to those that the gene police had accidentally omitted, and then to everybody," Mot began to describe an awful picture. "People walked the streets and persuaded themselves how good and humane was the state system governing them."

Speax darkened the colors more. "They even gathered in groups in the squares on their own initiative and shouted without reason, 'The system is just! The system is just!' This was a triumph of democracy. Were they insane? No. Their idea of normalcy was simply replaced and reduced to masochism. One suggested to oneself with joy, 'I need no rights! I want no rights!'"

"And he shared those thoughts with others. And they congratulated him," Mot offered, smiling wryly.

"He needed no rights! And, really, why should he need them?" Khoren derided. "He had all the rights ready in his brain, fed by the computer chip directly into his imagination—they were just rewritten from the Charter of the Rights of Man."

"This thrusting in the brain was a marvelous penetration of the State's long hand everywhere, totally. Quick, easy, and, what is most important, cheap! *Cheap!* Do you understand?" Speax said with a touch of emotion.

"Speax, this is cruel!" Paulo jumped up, shuddered, and began to pace the room. He was aghast by the slaying speeches of all his tutors on the one hand and this fit of emotion, otherwise strange for them, on the other.

"Cruel? But this is nothing," Speax replied as before, a bit emotional. "With this biochip, your own identity is eroded. The State can completely wash your brain, erase your memory, and you can lose your self-consciousness. It can change your Ego and inculcate into you quite another Ego. And then the identity 'I equals I' won't exist, the equality 'A equals A' won't be possible, and, thereby, idealism won't be possible at all. But, along with it, materialism will vanish, too. For matter itself will become senseless for you after it no longer is reflected in your consciousness, which will be changed beyond recognition—'I' will be different from 'I.' 'I' will not equal 'I.' The identity 'I equals I' will be dropped, as that absolute authentic first principle, which, according to the philosopher, is necessary to start towards reason. It won't be that unconditional truth as the basis necessary for the systematic form called science. Science? In this case, it is also lost in total futility. Then only Fichte's second basic identity will remain true, already also as unconditional, and no longer as a derivative—'I equals not I,' as well as 'not I equals I,' as a consequence and apology of the *absolute truth*—the State! Then man will be discussed only as a collection of atoms, as an aggregate of organic molecules and chemical reactions into which he could be decomposed when necessary and where necessary as an ordinary biomass for tests."

Speax stopped talking for a while. Paulo was upset by this tirade about the decline of man as a variant of his evolution, in which philosophy was adduced as a basis.

"I want something to drink," wished the novice. He poured himself a glass of some type of juice and said low-spiritedly, "That sounds so sad, my friends."

Speax had to finish his narrative. He went on, but now with his usual composed air. "So, Eternal Peace had at last been established. It was a peace born out of violence. There was prosperity; a prosperity born out of indifference. And prosperity that at any moment gave birth to indifference. And 'indifferent bodies, which touch each other, mutually strive to originate in themselves a decrease in cohesion.' Remember—Schelling. What do you think? Was he right that reason is the absolute thing? That outside of reason there is nothing, and everything is in it? You will become convinced that this is true if you fall among the general and full ignorance of this super technotronic civilization where the domination of vulgarity and idiotism over human reason was accompanied at the same time by the super-high development of artificial intelligence. These were paradoxes unexplained and unexplainable by their scientific academies, while in fact they were sharp, rending contradictions of an agonizing, decayed society."

Speax stopped speaking and passed the baton to Pat.

"The technologies overpowered man! Drug-addiction had no dangerous proportions. It was massive—by all people! The world of illusions, the world of hallucinations, had become for them a world of shadows, an after-life. But not as life after death, it was death during life."

"Drugs created calmness, the police created security," Khoren stipulated, joining in the conversation. "And there were no conflicts either. Calmness and security, as a result of philistine prosperity and indifference."

"Yes, technologies overpowered man, the spirit of man!" Mot added, continuing the common thought. "Each impulse for a rebellion was nipped in the bud. No one wanted freedom any longer. No one asked childish questions any longer. This was the agony of a whole society at the background of a seemingly general material satiety and security—the result of super technological industrialization."

"Man wasn't a wolf to man any longer," Pat pointed out, taking part in the discourse again. "It was worse—man was nothing to man. Despite all warnings to the scientists concerning this danger, they didn't grasp it in time; or they didn't wish to grasp it. And the last cry for help sank amid scientists' closet satisfaction. Simply, they even outpaced all other people in this respect."

“They had turned into money-making machines in science,” Khoren generalized. “And many of them, in fact the prevailing part, were not even scientists, but simply plagiarists and pseudo-scientists. They served only for direct and live processing of the doubting men in the system with the purpose that they should not become heretics—like television and police, by the way.”

Speax went on with Khoren’s thought. “Physicians, cybernetists, biologists, chemists, and geneticists were all appropriated by the State and served its interests. But in so doing, they didn’t serve society. They all were different in rank only in the State’s hierarchy, subjected to politics but not to science. Prominent minds in different areas of knowledge, scientists awarded prestigious awards, yet they couldn’t see, couldn’t grasp the transparent, simple truth that they were victims and only tools in different political games and machinations, that they were stooges of the political schemes of others, even as non-party, *impartial* citizens of the State.”

“This vegetation of society would have continued up to its final decomposition, to its nearing inevitable death,” Mot contributed, “if it hadn’t come somewhat earlier. Some member of the ruling family wanted to seize the power of the State entirely in his hands. He declared himself against the tyranny of the odious satraps—his relatives!—like a *fighter for freedom*, like a *revolutionary*, a *defender of democracy*.”

“And then, in the apocalypse of the star war, the planet was destroyed by this internecine war. It was a real space disaster, which tore the planet into countless small pieces, turning it into the asteroid belt of its star,” Speax finished the common narrative.

A short pause ensued, in which Paulo made sense of the entire story and Speax’s last words.

“Wait … wait a minute,” he uttered slowly, “but this story is the spit and image of the hypothesis of Phaeton, the tenth planet of the Solar system that orbited between Mars and Jupiter,” ejaculated the youth.

“Maybe it is. It may be everyone. Its name doesn’t matter. The other thing does,” was Speax’s answer.

"But is it indeed that planet?" insisted Paulo.

"Well, okay, it is," confirmed the master. "A piece of it once smashed into Earth, actually. But what do you know about this?"

"I know that this hypothesis logically linked in a whole so many otherwise empirical facts. However, according to the hypothesis, the blow that knocked Phaeton out of its orbit and pitched a piece of it towards Earth was due to a fatal collision with an unknown ominous comet. Now I understand that that is not quite correct. And if I try to associate this hypothesis with your words of a while ago with the help of my imagination, it will show an interesting pattern."

"Okay, we're listening to you."

"So, more than 11,500 years ago on the planet Phaeton, lived a civilization that was exceptionally highly developed in technology but not in social aspects. There were kindled imposing, planetary hostilities because of a sudden outburst of a global social conflict. The war carried into space, too. This war entered an uncontrollable phase of total mutual destroying of all bases, and the blows were so powerful that they split the planet into dozens of thousands of parts."

The student vividly showed the entirety of his hypothesis on the hologram.

"This had been an awful disaster. It had been the most grandiose, the most monstrous disaster in the Solar system! And the most sinister warning to Earth's mankind!" The young man shook his head, lost in thought, as if talking more to himself than the others.

"Only an insignificant part," he went on, "less than one percent of Phaeton's planet mass, was left to fly in its previous orbit—those small fragments from the upper layers, close to its surface, and having less density. Thus, the asteroid belt of the Solar system was formed. Astronomers' observations prove that, for all the asteroids to move in the same direction in space and with the same axis spinning around, it couldn't happen by an accidental collision. And, indeed, it hadn't been accidental. The splitter blow on Phaeton had been directed thus and so mightily, though maybe not intentionally, that it seemed as if this tearing-to-pieces destructive force had been caused by the tidal pull of an enormous heavenly body—after such tearing, all planet's remnants have the same direction in space and spin around only one axis."

"Why do you think so?" Mot asked.

"Because, only in this artificial way could all those pieces transforming into asteroids spin around only one axis with a fixed direction in space."

"Well, fire ahead," Speax smiled.

"If some asteroids remained turning in their previous planetary orbit, other pieces with bigger masses had been scattered in all possible directions, and some of them had been naturally developed self-dependent elliptic orbits. In this way appeared both the closest frequenter of the Sun, Ikarus, and the furthest one, Hyron, as well as all the others. Scattering like detonating shell-splinters, large pieces of rock flew off everywhere into the whole Solar system. On their way, they bombarded all the planets, forming closed-meshed nets of craters on them. At the passing of many such rock leavings, beside Mars for example, two of them 'hitched' onto it, caught by its gravitation, and transformed into its two satellites—Phobos and Deimos. Proof of that is not only in their unusual appearance, which is identical to the asteroids, but also in their internal composition and texture, density, dimensions, and mass. For example, Phobos belongs to the same class as the Trojan asteroids, a class that represents eighty percent of all asteroids—the so-called *carbonated chondrites*, the darkest cosmic bodies in the Solar system. And really, Phobos absorbs ninety-five percent of the light falling on its surface, just like these chondrites, as if it's torn from the same mass as they are."

All of this academic council kept a close watch on their student's exposé, as though silently agreeing with him. Paulo threaded the cosmic events as he saw them in his mind.

"However, it wasn't Mars alone. Thus had been caught *all* satellites by all planets in the Solar system beyond Mars—Jupiter, Saturn, Uranus, and Neptune. Except the rock fragments that bombarded the planets and all the other pieces with comparatively large masses which flitted by them, had been caught in the gravitation hug of the major planets, thus transforming these pieces right off into their satellites. Jupiter acquired seventeen satellites, and Saturn obtained fifteen, as I know disposing data from 1989. But I'm sure that Jupiter's satellites, as well as Saturn's, are over two hundred for each of them—big and small bodies captured after the explosion by their gravitation. In the whole Solar system, there are totally hundreds of satellites still unknown to the earth science. So many of them have highly eccentric and inclined orbits, and many have retrograde orbits, all just because of this sudden colossal explosion.

"When one or several of such cragged wanderers stumbled on Roche limit of Saturn, its tidal forces broke them up into countless small fractions, transforming them into a nonpareil brilliant ring around the most beautiful planet, creating the most marvelous view for man in our space." The youngster demonstratively proved his subject with a note of emotion like an excellent student who had passed his examination.

All the scientific committee members nodded their heads silently in general approval.

"I see logic in your words," Khoren told him. "And what more do you think?"

"Well, Uranus and Neptune also captured their satellites, but fewer, because of, first, the nearness, the immediate proximity of Jupiter and Saturn to the event, i.e., the catastrophe, and second, on account of the rather mightier gravity masses of Jupiter and Saturn, which barred and limited the rolling stones from moving any further out.

"Two comparatively large rock pieces succeeded in evading all the gravity traps. One of the reasons is just their bigger masses and sizes, but other, the basic reason they weren't caught by the major planets, especially by Jupiter and Saturn, is the steep slope, the inclination to the ecliptic by which they flew away, seventeen degrees. After they had 'run away' past the other outer planets, they went on their way trying to 'escape' the pull of the Sun too, but with no success—it didn't allow them to leave. Since the two fragments of rock didn't succeed in leaving the Solar system, they remained in it as its outermost planet, Pluto, and its satellite, Charon."

"To be more precise," Pat parenthesized, "this is a binary planet, Pluto-Charon, which turns around the barycenter of their orbits in view of the fact that the mass of Charon represents forty percent of Pluto's."

"Yes, you're right. It's a binary planet," the young scientist went on with his theory. "In its composition and texture, this binary planet is also identical to the asteroids. Just because it is kindred with them, these are all rocks of the planet Phaeton, which were torn off by the explosion. That is why only Pluto-Charon, among all planets, has an orbit with such steep gradient to the ecliptic—the couple is a 'fugitive' that was plucked off from the major planets, but not from the Sun! I'm sure Pluto has many more satellites of carbo-chondrites with even unthinkable macromolecules, such as proteins! I'm certain that beyond Pluto-Charon there are other planets, too, having even steeper gradients to the ecliptic, whose 'stampede' had been frustrating."

"What do you know about Iapetus and Phoebe?" Khoren was curious to know.

"Oh, thank you for the question," Paulo said, pleased. "Both of Saturn's moons corroborate my theory. They both have the same steep inclination to the ecliptic—Iapetus, more than seven degrees, and Phoebe, more than a hundred fifty degrees. Iapetus, as a smaller 'fugitive' than Pluto-Charon, was caught by Saturn's gravitation, which is why its orbit is unusual and is located strangely so far away from Saturn. Its shape is strange, too, just like an asteroid's. Phoebe's orbit is also strange, it's retrograde. But the albedo of these two satellites of Saturn just corroborates their common origin, their common outset. Phoebe's and Iapetus's albedos are very low because both are built of dark material, which consists of organic compounds. As far as I know, there is an assumption that Iapetus's dark material has its origin from Phoebe."

"Dark material with organic compounds on Phoebe and Iapetus? That's very interesting," Speax remarked provocatively.

"Not only on those two, there is organic material on Ceres as well as on many satellites in the whole Solar system, as I mentioned a while ago." The lad was warming up to the subject. "Yes, Ceres is the next proof, the proof positive of my hypothesis. Why? Ceres, the smallest planet and the biggest asteroid, contains the answer, if we look for a logical explanation of how, when, and from where it was able to acquire the largest quantity of liquid water in the whole Solar system! I mean, Ceres contains, sixty miles beneath its ice surface, two hundred million cubic kilometers of water, which is more than *all* of the fresh water on Earth! I'm speaking of a dwarf planet, which has a diameter of only seven percent of Earth's and a mass almost sixteen thousand times less than Earth's! And I highlight, we speak of *water*, the base of Earth life! In an amount that may be unique in deep space, too. Just like Pluto-Charon, Iapetus, and Phoebe, Ceres also has a steep inclination of over ten degrees! Ceres has a tenuous atmosphere of water vapors, rocks, and clay for the organic compounds' best development, and … a warm surface, despite its icy nature—only approximately minus thirty-six degrees Fahrenheit. Why, if Ceres is not a connate piece of a much bigger planet mass—this one of Phaeton?!"

"Let I add to you," Mot said. "Take a fact in your maintenance: on the asteroid Bennu there are traces of water, too. Your scientists will learn this fact very soon. Okay, what happened, however, inwards—to the Sun?" Mot put forth a question to the probationary member.

"Yes, tell me this: what happened inwards? I'd like to hear," Speax added in the ebullient monologue of the future brilliant scientist, nodding his head approvingly.

"There is other planet with a steep inclined orbit as a result of this common reason. This is Mercury," resumed the student. "A great part of large pieces of rock advanced towards the planets of the terrestrial group. Probably this was that part of Phaeton's nucleus, which shot in the direction of our luminary as shrapnel, as a super-speedy and mighty shell, accompanied by a shower of bigger and smaller rock pieces. It follows the bombing of the terrestrial planets, while the nucleus, flying past the star, lost a great part of its kinetic energy and fell into orbit around the Sun, transforming into the nearest planet to it—Mercury. This fact explains why it, the Lilliputian, has so strong magnetic dipole field—because this is, in fact, the nucleus of Phaeton, in contrast to the Moon, Mars, and the considerably bigger Venus."

"Yes, Mercury has a magnetic field commensurable only with Earth's," Khoren confirmed.

"It is no accident that it and only it serves exactly for a unit of measurement of Earth's magnetic field," Paulo picked up again. "That field was concentrated in that very mass, which was probably the most solid part of Phaeton's nucleus, in contrast to the weak magnetic fields of all other asteroids and satellites, similar to them, which had come from the upper layers of the planet. The same is the case with the solidity: 'unexpectedly large' for a planet with so small mass and commensurable—again!—only with Earth's. And of course, with Pluto having also a similar solidity! No matter how far distant they are, the first and the last planets are as two peas in a pod! And something more, an exceptional important proof about Mercury's origin from Phaeton is the fact that there are traces of an oxygen atmosphere on it, although they're trifling. An atmosphere in hell's oven!"

"You arranged very well, even excellently, the space puzzle in the Solar system up to now," the master Speax struck in again. "But Earth? Where did you put Earth?"

"Yes, Earth. But wait. I've just come to it. One, or a few, enormous pieces of flying crags, accompanied by a multitude of fine stones, a hailstorm of 'rubble,' was poured, as if by God's anger, on the humans' heads. They fell onto Earth, as well, like God's punishment, with frightful strength. What followed was a smashing blow, a shocking quake, which caused the sinking of two continents, which joined as an enormous one with an area as large as present day Europe, Asia, and Africa put together. It sank Atlantis. It was the Great Deluge. I know that when I was on Earth, a vast crater was discovered in Antarctica quite recently. It is more than three hundred miles in diameter and about two thousand and eight hundred feet in depth. The shock occurred there. It caused a large inclination in Earth's axis and dislocated the geographic poles and equator, which our unfortunate ancestors recorded then as came a large 'displacing of the stars.'

"That event led to a sharp change in the climate. Thereafter came the seasons of Earth. Straight away perished from frostbite the otherwise warm-loving mammoths, related to the elephants—some of them while still feeding!—since their south until that time native land of Jacutia, in which they lived, suddenly became ice-bound because of the terrible northern subpolar cold. There is much proof that China and Egypt in times gone have been equatorial areas—the Egyptian water clocks are almost as precise as atomic ones and work only in the latitude of the equator, the Chinese star globe that betrays an equatorial sky, and other such things."

Speax watched his student very intently, astonished by unexpected deep subtlety and logical thought of the youngster. He was more than pleased with his disciple. As if witnessing the event back in that time, Paulo went on with his hypothesis, almost falling into a trance.

"Earth's civilization perished. My God, when I just think for a while, it was much, much more than a tragedy! Ten billion tragedies gathered in one! It was really the end of the world! Screams, horrors, helplessness ... First, the collision itself. I can't ... I can't imagine such a shock—to turn Earth upside down! The sky staved in as if gaping at Hell! After that—the Deluge! The waters rushed in with huge waves, several miles high (!), and swept all away—they flooded whole continents! All people became fully hopeless. It began with intense volcanic activity—incessant sinister eruptions of hundreds of volcanoes with rumbling roars. It is chronicled that a dense, dusky fog wrapped the planet. The ground underfoot began to move: together with the fall of the ocean bottom, a reverse process was implemented, too—the rising up of mountains and ridges. Those mountains left under the water formed by their peaks the contemporary islands and archipelagos—the Azores, Hawaii, Iceland, Easter island... In general, it caused impetuous volcanic and tectonic activity.

"And all the while an incessant flood of stones was raining from the sky—those rock pieces accompanying the big fragments that entering the atmosphere have been transformed into luminous fires. This scene, according to eyewitnesses, looked as if 'new suns were kindled, which afterwards fell on Earth, bringing death and destructions. The universe was blanketed by darkness.' It was the Apocalypse! For real! Earth opened up—even in the literal sense. The shock was so hard that it caused a splitting of Earth's crust, which led to the appearance of the contemporary geo-magnetic anomaly zones—the Bermuda Triangle next to Florida and the Devil Sea next to Japan. These are right the places where the crust of Earth was split. Since then they left as enormous 'raw wounds,' I mean unlocked leaks that suck in and swallow up all that falls into their zones at certain times of raised activity. Even to this day, the open leaks are continuously gushing out, streaming, really as if from raw wounds in Earth's body, magma, which engenders warm streams in the oceans, the Gulf Stream for example. The young and tender, short-lived, human civilization became extinct. Nearly all people perished. A few of them were saved and began afresh in the east Balkan lands and, much later, in Sumer, Egypt, and India.

"Thus, in the last reckoning, this cosmic billiard game led to the contemporary form of the Solar system and a jolting cataclysm in human history. If we add up the total mass of all these planets—Mercury, Pluto-Charon, the satellites of Mars, Jupiter, Saturn, Uranus, and Neptune, as well as all asteroid belts, we'll get the real mass of Phaeton. Phaeton! ... Its ruin had been not only *its* ruin! But misfortune never comes alone." Paulo arranged the cosmic puzzle.

"And what's the conclusion then?" Speax addressed him.

"The conclusion, in the final reckoning, is that such a catastrophe must not be allowed to happen again. Because, besides itself, some civilization could destroy life in other places as well, and that is the bigger evil. And this means that you are certainly right—social conflicts are always due precisely to the State and money. The violence, leading in the long run to the suicide of society, is due to the State only. But I'd like to ask what happened to you when you passed beyond that dangerous boundary? I mean, I'm interested in how it goes with the other variant—when the civilization is not degenerated but continues to prosper?" The tellurian continued with his questions.

"How did we proceed?" Khoren first began to answer. "At first, after we had already built this social order, only then, with all of us having equal rights, did we begin a mighty settlement of the near space, of our interplanetary system. This most likely contributed to our also discovering thermo-nuclear synthesis, which, along with this social order, led to a real flourishing of our civilization."

"We constructed a multitude of main and subsidiary stations all over the planets," Pat continued, "which were of use later as starting bases for building this space system, the one that you saw and that you're now in. The construction of this space complex went on for forty-eight-hundred of your years. I'm speaking of its completely finished state. Otherwise, after the first sixteen hundred years, although the complex was still not so developed and completed, we could already travel freely, could *walk* in the near cosmos. But, in very deep space, we could scarcely advance when our artificial system was finished. From far back, we have had craft that can fly close to the velocity of light. With these craft, we can penetrate cosmic space with a radius of action up to about nine-hundred-sixty of your light years, that's to say nearly three hundred parsecs."

"However, these spacecraft models are already old, and we now use them for short transitions only where they're advantageous," Mot specified. "Besides that, we have other craft, improved, which reach a velocity of up to ten or even a hundred times higher than the old ones. That means we're not twenty-one hundred feet per second slower than the light, but actually flying just two hundred feet, even twenty feet, behind it."

"But parallel with this," Speax went on with the topic, "we also use other ways of moving faster in order to get where we want to go far away in space. We find the advantage in a velocity faster than light's. For that purpose, we use the gravity potential of the space-time continuum. Obtaining energy by the folds of the time and space, we can reach various remote galaxies outside ours. For example, in order to reach the neighboring galaxy that you call Andromeda, you'd need four-point-six million of your light years for going and returning, but we do this in four years only, while these four years are equal of one our year."

"Here, amongst you, nothing could surprise me anymore. Even that!" the Earth man replied, somehow mentally broken by this might. "I won't ask you this time how you do it, because the meaning won't be clear to me. However, I'm now convinced in the rightness of the ancient Egyptians about this matter, which seemed like stark fancy to me before. In *The Egyptian Book of the Dead*, the Egyptian priests quite clearly wrote about that thing which has 'swiftness higher than the light.' It's strange from where at their allegedly primitive, almost wild existence, along with all the other countless fantastic and improbable fundamental knowledge, the priests had learned that light has, first, *swiftness*, i.e., **velocity,** something that was established by our modern science scarcely in the nineteenth and twentieth centuries. Second, that it's a **frontier,** a kind of limit, accepted for comparing all velocities. And third, to have clear awareness that they knew exactly what that thing was that was faster than light."

"Indeed, from where?" Speax smiled mysteriously and stood up. All four of Paulo's tutors left their disciple to take a rest.

11

On this planet, Paulo did not see one woman; that does mean that there was no one man, either. These humans were asexual beings. They lived eternally, although not infinitely. After a period of sharp sprawling of the planet's population through sexual selection, there followed a discontinuation of the inhabitants' number increasing, just like the evolution of the human brain. Perhaps after a long time, the galactic "brain" will follow the model of the human one and planetary one, what the Omeronean society was—at a certain stage in their evolution, the neurons stop to multiply, they discontinue their reproduction in contrast to all other cells, the somatic ones, which on Omeron the various robots represented. It seems this evolution is coded into the genetics of Life.

At first Paulo felt himself in a maze. He was startled by the fact that, here, genetic reproduction had stopped; here there was not any regenerative potential. Children were not born here. For life's duration was equal to millennia. Yet, if any human did die, his place in the information brain's activity of the society was immediately filled by a bio-robot, who differed in no way from his noble predecessor, except that he did not have "blue blood," i.e., he was born in a laboratory.

For an Earth man, this was in every respect a strange and completely unaccustomed world.

These humans somehow looked not so solid, not so heavy, pale, and faintly gauzy. This civilization was like an odd society of yogis; yogis slightly lucent at times. They had a transparent blood, the oxygen in it was transported directly, without hemoglobin. This fact contributed them feeling very well under low for the terrestrial temperatures that was maybe a necessity into the wide cosmos. They had a very low body temperature, could go without meals for a very long time, and had no need to urinate—these were serious factors for their long, centuries-old life. A man from Earth could not explain to himself whether they had a metabolism; probably yes, but what kind?

These humans communed directly among themselves without vesting their thoughts with words of spoken speech. It was not necessary—they used telepathic contact. And because of that, they all understood each other through one "language" only. All people could discuss all subjects without need of interpreters, without a language barrier as a result of national borders. The lack of speech as a mediator, the lack of need for thought to be obligatorily converted into speech, to be transformed into sound, had led to communication that could not put forth a lie, a fraud, stealthy intrigues, and would not contain hypocrisy and falseness. There was no dissimulation, villainy, or insidiousness, because every man read the thoughts of every other one like the literal truth. In this civilization, social life was taking place by a direct exchange of energy—without money, as well as direct exchange of information—without speech, united in a common info-energy exchange. In this way, through telepathic contact, every man could deliver and receive messages and realize direct information connections to thousands of miles and with millions of correspondents without any communication equipment. And this fact allowed people to increase these direct contacts as working relations extraordinarily up to tens of thousands of times. Every man knew and had business contacts, not just with a close circle of persons, but with ten million to one billion people; however, he could have such contacts with an unlimited number of them, practically with all. But it is namely nerve links, nerve nets, which determine the intellect of a brain. What is important is not the number of nerve cells, but the number of their links!

Here the human brain could exercise fantastic functions, and the human had become unrecognizable. Besides telepathy, there was the mass practice and development of telekinesis, hypnosis, and all those miracles of the brain, which on Earth were once rejected as pseudo-scientific, as circus art. If some weight needed to be shifted, every man made it happen with a look, without any difficulty. If there was a need somewhere during their expeditions far away from Omeron, with a look only, i.e., with the power of his brain, every man could stop or start all kinds of mechanisms—rough and super weighty as well as fine and nearly weightless, including huge appliances and small ones. It was possible for every man, for example, to stop an imposing old-generation computer, a running escalator, or a car, as well as put in motion a stopped micro-clock or radio receiver, and also to obviate failures of space equipment, and that from very long distances.

The science of the brain had perhaps reached its peak, its apogee, its utmost possible acme of perfection. For, unlike the terrestrials, who used only 4 to 12 percent of their brain's capacity (geniuses only up to 20 percent), these humans here used their brain's full capacity, 100 percent. This very fact made superfluous any machine or device or the like for the entire existence of every individual. From the point of view of this Earth man, everyone here was a physician, an engineer, a worker, or what not—in fact, all of them. Every human was an all-around person. Every man had universal possibilities like all others. Every individual used his brain in a way that was needed at every given moment. Or, perhaps, to be more precise, every brain used itself, i.e., its own unlimited phenomenal possibilities, depending on circumstances. For example, if a precise medical checkup of the internal organs was needed, there was no need for heavy and primitive X-ray apparatuses. Through only a new tuning of the emitting state of the brain, every human of this planet could see the viscera of the other one facing it, just like on an X-ray photograph. After that, the miracles with healing occurred autogenously, with self-adjustment, or through the hands of the healer who granted health via his bio-field—without pills or operations.

These ethereal creatures tuned their brains in alpha-waves and rested only thirty minutes in a twenty-four-hour period, if we use terrestrial measures. Four hours of dream-time were equal to fifteen minutes of concentration on this alpha-rhythm.

This short meditation had replaced the otherwise prolonged eight-hour dream. It meant exceptional working capacity of each individual, and of the society as a whole. In fact, in twenty-four hours they could work twenty-four hours. For these thirty minutes of rest were also work—processing and filtrating all stored information up to that moment. So, in practice, this planetary brain worked incessantly, just like the human one.

In a lateral view, however, these humans looked very strange when they were wrapped up in themselves in their calm postures, as strange as all other things here, by the way. In such a moment they resembled mummies—unfathomable and alien. In this condition, these unusual creatures looked like dead—with closed eyes, immovable and cold, they could be taken for wax figures. The "bedroom" in this case was something like a wax-work exhibition. When Paulo saw Speax in this trance for the first time, he was strongly startled by his dreadful appearance. But he was sensible enough to guess that this condition was a "dream," that Speax was deeply "sleeping," and he must not disturb him.

However, even the bravest visionary's dreams could not vie with this reality. For these humans could fly! Yes! Besides all the other miracles, they could surmount gravity, too. And again, it was thanks to the brain! Along with all the other miracles, they mastered levitation as well. Whenever Paulo looked up to the outside, he saw how these humans-birds soared calmly and freely everywhere in the surrounding space. Without any flying machines! Just like that—by body only! But with certainty in spirit, too! These humans could fly thousands of miles. They did not need any technical conveyances or any means of communication for that. Everyone could establish direct contact with everybody else in every nook of the planet or fly there through his brain only. The brain was all; the brain could do all.

"Oh, my God! Am I dreaming?" Paulo reiterated to himself incessantly. "Who'd believe me? They'll take me as a mad probably. They'll throw me in a mental facility if I dare to share all this with someone on Earth. Flying people! As a poetic figure, as an allegory—yes, but as a reality… Good God! To what an amazing extent they master energy! Unbelievable! There is simply nothing impossible for them from our point of view."

Paulo had learned that these flights in waking state, in which, however, the flying people were as if blissfully fallen into a sleeping state, had not always been their natural condition. In the beginning, the great successes of the super-conductivity in the good old times had led to the creation of anti-gravitation bracelets, the assistance of which people could use to make similar flights. But subsequently even these bracelets dropped off when the brain had become all. This is a kind of sleep-walking, but acquired and steerable. This is the highest form of somnambulism, in which the "sleeping" man also must not be startled. Then Paulo remembered that on Earth he had also seen something similar, but there were only funny jumps by a few people, and it was possible only for them, a handful of elects. Yes. This was a demonstration of a group of yogis –in the United States, maybe in New York or Washington. The youth even remembered the year—1986. Three years only before he had "set out" for here.

On a magazine's cover, he saw a photo of smiling young people who rose in the lotus pose about two feet above the ground in front of the astounded eyes of the gathered spectators. They had tuned themselves in to some still dormant brain rhythm. The proviso was to keep absolute silence, because even the faintest noise, the faintest sound, could break up their concentration, which would lead, not so much to wounding them as they fell to the ground, as much as to a failure of the trial. The spectators did not believe their eyes, while the white-haired old Hindu, who was their Teacher, prophesied distant times for a reality that was already here, on Omeron. A man flying in the expanse on his own! Who would think this possible?

The brain's possibilities were quite unsuspected, unrecognizable, and unthinkable for a low intellectual creature like the man from Earth. Even a high-voltage current was completely harmless for these otherwise frail beings. One could, without trouble, thrust his naked hands in a device with fifty thousand volts of tension and no damage would be done, not even a scratch. Such occurrence on Earth was a sensation, and science kept silent, perplexed.

They had no theater, because they had no aspirations for any art of public speaking, simply because they did not use speech for communication among themselves.

They had no music, because everything was music. They did not play it, but perceived it directly from everything and from everywhere, just like deaf Beethoven near the end of his life—he felt it with his very being, with all of his brain, i.e., as mathematics and logics, but not as sound. The audible spectrum of sound waves is tiny compared to the entire range of vibrations. They imbibed the highest musicality that is emanated by the perfect harmony of the highest order of the Universe. Was Einstein also not right in this respect when he searched for musicality in each discovery, in each new blade of science? Music as emanation but not as sound.

These nondescript supermen, almost imperishable and soaring in the air like biblical angels, were afraid of absolutely nothing. No fear, even of death. Not because they were not acquainted with it. Perhaps it came to them, although after thousands of years. They looked perennially young. But they did not know fear, because they could not feel this emotion. Simply, they had no right hemisphere in their brains or, to be more precise, they had it, but during evolution it had been stunted and rolled up as a little ball to the extent that it was hidden, enveloped by the left hemisphere, which took up the capacity of the whole brain-pan. For that reason, these humans felt practically no emotions. It may be strange, it may even be terrible from the point of view of Earth man, but they hardly evinced any emotions. They were completely different people. They were changed beyond recognition and represented some perfect bio-computers. Surely, it seems cruel, but the evolution required this of them. It was required by the higher organization of matter, as their civilization was. For God continuously proves that really It is a mathematician. This state is a psychological barrier that the terrestrial man could hardly overcome. From an emotional point of view, he cannot and does not want to adapt that state as normal in other rational beings, which is normal for the other. And quite naturally, these states are different levels of evolution, and they cannot mingle. But everything flows, nothing stays the same. Could the Australopithecus adopt the way of life of the modern man as normal with much more reason compared to him, with much more rationality and less emotion? That is why it is no accident that fear is strongest in the primate, less in the reasoning man, and missing in the cosmic one. So, it is quite natural that, on their higher level of rationality, these humans almost could no longer feel any emotion as a normal way of life, and it is quite natural for terrestrial man to be emotionally indignant at this and unable to adopt it as normal. But from the unicellular to the human, in every next advancing species, the Creator put into it more and more rationality and effectiveness. That is why this society, although compounded by people perfect bio-computers, was a manifestation of the reason as a form of life, but not of the indifference as a form of death. These people either had to perish or change to this appearance. And what was the way toward this survival? The difference between good and evil—this is the supreme ethical standard, which must be put into the program of each reason just so, as the difference between 1 and 0, between true and false—in order to keep self-destruction out of it. When this difference is obliterated, certain death always comes.

The time in the Universe for this space constitution flew much more quickly, and it was perceived in quite a different way—not just like a Universe, but like a much smaller world. For the ocular perception, which outlines the borders of the world surrounding a certain reason, was quite different. The same physical reality could be seen in different ways. No animal sees the world as the man does, although it is the same for them. It is the same manner for man in the case of the cosmos. The Cyclops "eyes" of this stellar stranger were ten thousand times more powerful than man's, i.e., they had "pupils" (let's call them) ten times bigger than the biggest telescope on Earth, which is three-hundred-thirty feet in diameter. The otherwise endless heretofore cosmos was exceptionally diminished now. The otherwise desert, dead, heretofore cosmos, was suddenly animated now. However, watching with these "eyes," it turned out that precisely this world was real for this biological unit, the planetary reason, which was filling the next higher stage in life's evolution after man. It was precisely this world, but not that one which we, the terrestrials, are seeing; it was not stagnation, but a world filled with life. It was not a frozen, immovable world, but an incessantly moving one. In the space ocean, some galaxies looked like its waves, which swelling across each other, during colossal high tides, at their collisions took away, tore off from each other, swarms of stars and galactic gas. And after that, at the low tides, as veritable ocean waves again, they rolled back, scattering hydrogen gas by themselves and left it like spreading sea foam on the beach. Spiral galaxies were seen, which spun quickly like childish, fair whirligigs or maybe more precisely, like vortical cyclones; supernovas that flashed briefly, flared up like the lights of fireflies; quasars pulsating like lighthouses; explosions of whole galaxies or galaxies connected by stellar bridges. In general, it was seeing how the entire world looked from an upper degree. The events of space now ran stunningly fast in comparison to the customary man's observations from Earth, but in this world they were perceived as quite normal, ordinary, i.e., not as relative. The physics in it was Newton's once again, and the geometry, Euclidean. Only the transition to the other, more embracing Universe, which envelops ours and which appears for it as Cosmos, occurred according to the laws of relative mechanics.

12

Such was the reality that surrounded the planetary reason of Omeron. Life on this planet was radically different in every way compared to life on Earth. Indeed, everything around was material, but it was so perfect and fine that it shaded the ideal of a lower intelligence such as the earth. The entire world surrounding the tellurian guest was material, in fact, but it was so ethereal and so far remote from our crude proto-ideas of matter that it was losing this sense and reaching for an inaccessible ideal. Everything is only moving matter, indeed, but it is an ideal and remains ideal for each of its lower organizations of movement. There comes a time when this frontier—the frontier between material and ideal things—is merely lost, i.e., when the material substance shades off into an ideal one.

Paulo lay on his bed and speculated precisely on these subjects.

Probably the so-called astral body is, in fact, energy matching mass of the corporeal body of every living constitution. The Law of the conservation of energy is evinced especially well here. At the moment of death of every living constitution, the astral body departs the corporeal one like a little bit, usually invisible, light cloud. A little bit, because of the exceptionally little, trifling quantity of pure energy, which matches the mass of the dying body. Light, because the light is the sole connection between them, between the energy (astral) body and the corporeal one. And one who has seen this little bit of cloud is thinking that he has seen the departing soul of the dead man. But, in fact, this is his or her energy moving away from the body at this moment. The aim and the sense of this movement are, for the astral body, to settle again, to be regenerated in a new corporeal body. The soul has weight.

Yes, to a certain extent this is so. I could say so-so thus. Unexpectedly, from somewhere, Speax joined in his thoughts.

Paulo was already qualified for such kind of talk, using thoughts only by distance. Inconspicuously to him, Paulo already had begun to imbibe the thoughts of his patron with a look and transferred to him his own thoughts. He could not understand how Speax tutored him subconsciously in his mute language every day, every hour, every minute while they talked, ate, and while he slept. Only once had the young man dimly felt something similar. Speax was making him ready for that moment, impending and close, when these talks would be without words.

Speax, is that you? Great! I'd like to know, please, does this mean that the rebirth is, in fact, just this flight of energy this has already moved away from one body to another? That this is energy, carrying in itself at each settlement into a new form, coded data for the particular, specific features of the bygone life?

Yes, but this is possible only under the condition that the distance in space between these two bodies in this moment is especially close, not more than a few miles. That's to say, in a confined incidence. Otherwise the soul, i.e., the energy body, departs as a holographic copy in the common energy field of the system, in this case— the planet, and it reincarnates in a child between the ages of three and seven years old, not longer than two years later. The energy-information-field form of the matter could perceive, and mostly is perceived, exactly as an incorporeal 'ghost,' as a specter, for which the laws and borders imposed by its corporeal form are invalid. The ghost is the form, the holographic copy, of this energy-information-field matter, while the soul is the content, its character, its gene, Speax acknowledged.

Yes, I know that not one or two but many unbelievable facts about reincarnation filliped the science on Earth to search at last for a serious interpretation of them. Professor Stuart Edelstein, I think, from the University of Geneva, investigated tribes in Western Africa and described a number of instances in his book, the title of which I don't recall now, and American and Indian scientists have studied other similar cases in their countries. It turns out that there is not only a material but an energy genetic code, too, is that so? In other words, inherited information could be handed down, not only directly with a material bearer, but also from a distance with an energy one? Paulo added.

Exactly, Speax took up, *in contrast to the DNA molecule, which carries information from the past to the future development of the* ***body,*** *of man's physical cells, energy quanta, with a fixed frequency, carry information from the past to the future development of the* ***mind,*** *of the person's reasoning. This, taken as a whole, is what expresses the reincarnation or the rebirth. For you know that, first and foremost, only the mind is the man, but not the body. So, in such a case, you could really say that the body dies, but the soul is immortal. It's because energy really is immortal. It is always preserved, and it is exactly this property which enables it to be 'born anew' in the next man's body for the next life cycle.*

Speax paused a bit, and then continued. *Every physical system, such as the Solar system, and Earth in particular, consists of an integrated energy-information field, a united field compound of otherwise particular fields—electric, magnetic, gravitational, quark-gluon. Every man could take part in it in a different way and with a different aim—to fly in space like a bird, for example, or to 'speak' by thoughts only with another man who is widely separated from him. Of course, there must be a preliminary preparation.*

Bizarre results could be achieved by remote inherited information—species ranging from the most perfect to the most teratoid forms.

Yes, I've read something similar, Paulo broke into Speax' exposition. *Some living bio-system, for example an animal, is set in a box-receiver and is irradiated by a super high-frequency source. Its waves engrave the genetic information of the bio-system and later, irradiating some embryo, such as a bird's egg, conveys and puts it in the future growth of that embryo. Thus, omnifarious genetic hybrids could be produced—a cat with wings, for instance, or a rabbit with goatish horns, a chicken-duckling or corn-tree and whatnot.*

Yes, in this way all diseases could be cured, Speax picked up again. *Or it could create new ones. It could eradicate all physical infirmities and congenital defects, or it could 'redress' all mental 'defects' in the freedom-thinking man. It depends into whose hands this steerable heredity technique falls. If this is the reborn Dr. Mengele, he could meddle in the genetic code of men, animals, and plants and mutate the information written in their genes. Thus, this satanic affair could mutate God's gist of men, animals, and plants producing omnifarious, custom-made, chimera organisms.*

The genetic information could spread to a great distance, because every living biological system, which is situated in high-frequency and with a high tension electric field, emits its own weak field, which copies the quite precise delineations of all the constitution's parts, even those that are missing for one reason or another. For example, put a fresh leaf with a truncated top in such a field, and on its photo later, you'll see the whole leaf.

Yes, this is the Kirlian effect, the student ejaculated mentally.

That's right. You know this as the Kirlian effect. It is possible because of the fact that, besides the common genetic code, the chromosomes contain a strategic one as well. That means that, besides inherited information for the reproduction of some albumen, they also carry inherited information, which is recorded volumetrically as a holographic picture in the three spatial dimensions. In other words, a picture with detailed texture in the space, along with a circumstantial program for the whole constitution's development in the course of time. In this way, as in the case with the leaf, despite some part being missing on the holographic picture, the whole constitution is seen. This is the so-called phantom effect or Kirlian effect, as you know it.

Then the existence of such phenomena as clairvoyance, predicting the future, wreathed-in-mysticism fortune-telling and prophecy are possible only because of the existence of this united energy field and the personal program of everyone in it? Paulo asked.

Every man, as a part of the events in this field, carries with himself modulated in his bio-field, information about his own bio-program, in which is held all events in his life, and which can be deciphered only by super-sensitive bio-receivers. Because of the special tuning of their brains, only people receiving the respective waves with a fixed frequency could see the frames of this 'holographic' program. So, the phantom effect allows the clairvoyant to clearly see, as if on cine-film, the whole fate, i.e., the genetic information in spatial-time perspective in the program of the living biological system next to him, be it flower, bird, or human. That is why he has the faculty to identify both the kin of the man beside him and persons with whom this man has no acquaintance at all, persons who could be hundreds or thousands of miles away or just missing his blood relatives. Something more, the clairvoyant is even able to call the names of the dead relatives of this man, since the phantom effect, just like the leaf with the truncated top, allows everyone to emanate a bio-field, as I already mentioned. This bio-field precisely goes over the delineations of all constituent parts of the bio-system to which it belongs, in this case the kin, even if some of these parts are missing. Simply, the soothsayer joins with his brain in the united energy field of the system, and there succeeds in seeing the weak bio-field of the living organism standing close to him. This possibility allows him to carry on conversations with every living being around— plant or animal, with every blade of grass, every creature and bug, with daisy or crane. Speax ended his long and remote "speech."

But in this case, Paulo continued to speculate on his patron's words, *the life of each man is predestined, from birth to death! Each man has explicit behavior in the spatial-time segment in which he's placed. He can act precisely in a pre-determined way and only in this way. He is just as he is and he cannot be otherwise. This is his* ***fate,*** *from which, even if he wanted to, he cannot escape. It's his submission to fate. One* *vaguely feels through his senses this predestination, but he cannot explain it, can he?*

Yes, the fate is felt but not seen.

That is why Mozart and Tchaikovsky are great composers, but not physicists like Plank and Bore, for example. Dante created the nine circles of the dark, while Beethoven the nine symphonies of the light. But not vice versa.

Yes, all of them partake in the common code with a clear-cut individual task, a mission, not allowing casual mistakes or arbitrary actions. Everything is previously recorded—you'll be king, or you'll be Goethe!

Then, for that reason, the Vikings once believed in fate's full predestination and proceeded as warriors with great temerity. But the same fact could lead other people to slavish resignation. In such a case, where's free will left? Does not every man decide his fate himself? In this way the predetermination conveniently acquits the actions of every criminal!

Each event in the life of each individual, as a part of the common events in society, is programmed and fixed in time and spot, and there is no place for free will here. The fate of everyone is written as a sub-program of the common program. The free will is expressed solely in the ***realization*** *and* ***repentance*** *for the evil done if someone has been burdened with it. Otherwise, the Program, made by God, ensures equitable retribution for every evil, according to the crime, both in the present and the next biological life of the individual, as karma. The evil is programmed so far as it is karma; the evil must pull through to keep everything square.*

You mean that the fate of everyone is recorded as a computer program's algorithm, according to the significance of his deeds in the present life?

Yes, fate represents an algorithm of program with a multitude of **if-then** *cycles. I mean, karma is born each time a man reaches this dilemma in his actions—***if** *good,* **then** *happy and peace;* **if** *evil,* **then** *retribution and suffering. Here is the free will—if each man does his good, then society will be in harmony.*

I know that one of the seven Mayan prophecies is the same: either mankind will perish or the people will pass into full harmony between themselves and nature. Speax, after all our talks over so much time, I now feel initiated into the innermost secrets of the Universe. And I feel some void because of all Earth's vanity, concluded the terrestrial novice, and then he fell asleep.

13

Paulo's stay on Omeron lasted three years, which was equal to twelve Earth years. He could have remained longer, he could have remained forever, but he yearned to see Earth again, the people near and dear to him from whom he had so suddenly detached himself and moved away. What were they doing at this moment? Probably they did not even suspect what had happened to him and where he was now. What did Manuel say to them? And how did they take it?

Paulo had to return; he wanted to return. He was simply out of touch with his natural environment. His roots were calling him back. The young man had gained enough wisdom, yet now he had to share it. And there was not even a woman here, at least, who could fascinate his mind and give him a reason to stay on even a little longer.

Paulo had an impending departure. *Daring* had to set out again in two hours and would have to fly beside the Sun, too. When the two friends were off to the craft, Speax, silently directing his eyes to his guest, threw in: *Paulo, according your calendar, it is now the year 2012. In a week when you set foot on Earth again, it will be already 2023. Your planet won't be as you remember it.*

Indeed, how will Earth have changed in thirty-four years? What has happened on it? I wonder whether Faustus still believes in Mephistopheles.

14

The grandiose starship emerged as though from the nothing; it appeared as if suddenly from the black abyss and sharply increased its dimensions to those of a drifting iceberg or a flying mountain. The enormous cosmic bird jerked to slacken its speed to a rather low degree and took a path further placing it into orbit around the star.

Like chicks chased from their nests, coveys of dozens of space capsules flew away in the black vacuum from the three giant spheres of the craft, which headed impetuously for the planetary system of this star. It was the Sun.

Like an enormous formicary, a string of dozens of violet capsules filed one by one. Like bees from a hive, they had to gather *gas pollen* and light metals from the planets' surfaces. Some capsules, in one of which was Paulo, too, set a heading for Earth.

Until now, an Earth man had never seen with his own eyes the planets of his own solar system. This was an unforgettable experience. Flying alongside each one of them, Paulo felt the same emotions of rapture and flush as had welled up with all their might in the first men who flew in space or set foot on the Moon.

Speax expressly set the course thus that they could pass quite closely along the planets. Neptune stood in their way as huge blue, glassy pearl. It was the first blue planet of the Sun, and in a certain time it would probably have served as a boundary check-point to the system. On the blue face of the planet, the Great Dark Spot scudded, from which immense spurts broke away. Further down toward the South Pole, the youth set his eyes on the Small Dark Spot, alias The Wizard's Eye. Up to this moment, he did not know of Dark Spots' existence, and because of that he was left wondering and even astonished by this fact. Paulo did not know that the Small Dark Spot appeared and disappeared cyclically in the years, as well as that, in the northern hemisphere, there was another Great Dark Spot. But he likened at once the Great Dark Spot here to the Great Red Spot on Jupiter. They were similar in many ways. Inside his mind settled more and more deeply the suspicion that all large planets are, in fact, "pulverized drops" of a smaller twin of the Sun; that they are torn and broken, but still live solar matter. Weren't they all smoldering "coals" from the "embers" of a common star mass? Weren't all large planets remainders only from an ever-torn Sun's double component? What could be the reason for this? Perhaps it was a colossal tidal force from some exceptionally mighty galactic subject? But when might this have happened? Was it at the forming of the Sun five billion years ago? Or it was later, sixty-five million years ago? Maybe this was the reason for the dinosaur's perdition and the mass extinction of the life on Earth in general, during some millions of years. But along those same lines of thought, then the cosmic catastrophes in the Solar system probably became a minimum of two cases. First, the star-twin, and then the planet Phaeton also. In such a case of the *real* planets, i.e., those rocky ones, which are the result of real planet formation, only four remain: Venus, Earth, Mars, and Phaeton. It turns out then that the first Flood had been more fearful than the second one. In that case, is it possible to have a third one?

Concerning the perdition, concerning the tragic doom of Phaeton, Paulo no longer had doubts about that. A much greater number of satellites from the known, which he saw around Neptune, and subsequently around the other planet-giants, too, deepened his conviction more and more. Along with the belts circling about them, undeniable material evidence for this perdition was already for him. Of all these planets, only Saturn had succeeded in Roche limit to break into small pieces a lot more of the rock mass around itself in a belt just because it had this possibility. Belts, loose and slender, also existed further around Neptune and Uranus.

Speax did not intrude upon Paulo's thoughts. He let him reason calmly and did not take his conclusions as paradoxical. On the contrary, as logical and correct. During this time they flew past Pluto, which was numb in bluish ice and resembled a colossal cave with amazing forms spilled in titanic stalactites and stalagmites, miles in length, which the lovely freak of the pale light transformed into an unforgettable fairy sight. The ice crystals refracted and reflected the tired light beams in concentric colored circles. Its satellite, Charon, only supplemented the unique cold beauty. Obviously, the Sleeping Beauty was either not here or had not woken up yet.

Not long after cutting across the orbit of the green stranger Uranus, the astronauts found themselves in front of the magnificence and the proud, lofty mien of Saturn. The sight became more and more enthralling with their approach to the planet, especially beside Janus. Oh, my God, bless this moment! Bless the man stricken silent by this fascination! Give him fortitude, God, to support all its heaviness!

Poor boy, he was moved to tears by rapture subdued by His Majesty. With extremely open pupils, mute, and enchanted by all this witchcraft, the wretched youth watched with veneration the solemn procession before him. With a unique king's lordliness, Saturn stalked triumphantly, escorted by its multitudinous suite of moons, surrounded by the whole king's court. Not for anything in the world could Paulo take his eyes from its magnetic pageant and stood up enervate under its weight.

As he well expected, the singularities of the satellite Iapetus were due to the same causes that formed Eros. Their forms were similar, and their behavior, as well. Iapetus was not a *raft*, but was shaped more like a cigar, which explained the mysterious sharp alterations in its brilliance. Besides that, the asteroid's substance itself in some spots absorbed the light almost completely! Iapetus, together with Phoebe, had been built of so-called *dark material*, which absorbed the light, and their albedo was close to zero! Namely the origin of the dark material of Saturn's two satellites, and some others, was a mystery for Earth's scientists. In their opinion, Iapetus's dark material consisted of organic compounds, and they made a guess that this dark material was derived from Phoebe. And this meant they had a common origin! But what do we know about Phoebe? It's Saturn's satellite, rich in hydrocarbons and polymers! It's very strange! Besides that, there is frozen carbon dioxide on it, which is quite alien for all the asteroids' substance. Still more strange! Finally, Phoebe's texture is fifty percent rocks, while the inner satellites' rocks are only up to thirty-five percent. Why? All of this betrays the remains of an inhabitable planet in times long ago. Something more, Iapetus's orbit inclination of almost eight degrees, as well as Phoebe's of nearly one-hundred-fifty-two degrees(!), just repeated the sinister initial cause for the inclination of Pluto and Mercury! All of them could only be the debris of the shattered planet Phaeton.

Not with the idea to astound his terrestrial friend with the technical possibilities of the space capsule, but to give pleasure to him before the forthcoming parting, Speax abruptly headed for Cassini's Crevice. The planet rose up to its full height and filled the entire horizon, a vast motley mass divided into strips. Since they had descended from the pole to the equator, uppermost Saturn had a greenish color, which in the lower latitudes gradated to orange-yellow. Down the tropic, near the equator, the yellow color shaded almost into white. At this moment, the capsule dipped headlong through the crevice and passed below the ring. It was a marvelous scene of fairy colors! From a distant perspective, the variegated rug of the planet in aureate and orange was in harmony with a reseda color and fit wonderfully as decoration into the colors' common play that also came from the rings. It was an indescribable kaleidoscope with all tints of the rainbow! Rough ice chunks and blocks, not very big, jostled over their heads with blind strength and disorder. Paulo stood charmed in ecstasy.

Leaving Saturn far away, the capsule continued on its way. Inside, all passed in the same manner as Paulo had remembered from the very first day—no noise or speech. The eight astronauts of the crew silently discharged their duties as before, communing on and off with active looks at each other.

Now this style of communion did not seem so dreadful and so strange to Paulo. It was not even humdrum, because now he too participated in their mute conversations.

In about forty minutes, the distance of four-hundred-million miles was overcome. However, quite unexpectedly, there appeared unforeseen disturbances in the engine. Even this equipment could fail! Paulo thought it was more than ideal, because, until now, he had never witnessed anything similar. It never crossed his mind that something could jam. He felt so sure, and there was a reason. But although exceptionally rarely, once in a hundred million times, this event, nevertheless, could occur. These men—gods themselves—were still men, although gods!

To eliminate the engine trouble, the crew undertook an emergency landing on Ganymede, Jupiter's largest moon. Speax singled out a vast and level place, which very much resembled the dried-up bed of a sprawling high-water river. The ground was deeply cracked. On both banks towered medium-high hills, which consisted of large stone blocks that seemed to have been thrown sweepingly about and which looked like mountain screes.

The picture that opened out from here was worthy only of the greatest artist's palette. Jupiter! Its grandiose disc, filling up almost the entire horizon, inspired colossal might, monstrous power, in front of which one had to bend the knee! If Saturn was the king of the planets, Jupiter was the emperor! His temple on Capitol has to be shifted here! Jupiter the Thunderer! Just what storms raged, what lightning streaked this giant! Its whole length was woven by parti-colored belts, lighter and darker, which moved with different speed according to its place from the equator toward the pole, and in different directions, too. The motley variety of colors, being discrete in zones and stripes, very much resembled in combination the colorful embroidery of Bulgarian folk dress. And this eye! The Great Red Spot! As an enormous, bloodshot eye of an irate god, it was as if watching from above what occurred on his satellite, Ganymede. Jupiter, viewed from here, looked slightly inclined with its equator to the right, and this eye that watched them incessantly situated as though hanging above the heads of the uninvited newcomers. These atmospheric whirlwinds with elliptic slips impressed the human mind unusually strongly.

Just at this moment, Paulo was in a position to see an interesting phenomenon. Coming nearer to the Red Spot, the Great South Disturbance bent close to it, sharply increasing its speed while skirting it, whereupon it slowed down when it had moved away from the dangerous whirlwind. The Red Spot's dynamic equilibrium always persisted.

Paulo knew that Jupiter was a place filled with mysteries. Its unexplainable "broadcastings" strongly puzzled Earth's scientists. What was the nature of this powerful radio signal being emitted every nine hours fifty-five minutes and 29.37 seconds? What was the nature of the other half dozen weaker radio signals coming from its surface? What sort of activity were they all manifestations of? An activity of intelligence? Or of fortuity?

The most stunning fact of all, however, was Io's shadow. At that moment, the satellite was located overhead to the right at a stone's throw from the planet. Its shadow was a little black circlet on Jupiter's cloudy atmosphere. Just there the temperature was fifty degrees, not lower, but higher than the adjacent areas! Scarcely fifteen minutes after the shadow's displacement the temperature returned to normal! How was it possible that this midget, this gnome, influenced a god in this way? Why does this "mole" throw the scientists into perplexity and put science to the test?

Paulo's train of thought was broken, because suddenly the capsule swept up and flew off into space. Obviously, the engine trouble was repaired.

They cut across the asteroid belt. The pitiful remains of a global tragedy! The ashes of one civilization! A diadem of man's madness and covetousness! Thousands of scattered stones rolled in common order, solitary and sorrowful, keeping within themselves millions of ghastly secrets.

The space in front of them became more and more bright. The dark increasingly dispersed. They had already passed Mars's orbit and were less than five minutes to Earth. All four tutors of Earth's newly initiated into the cosmic secrets were surrounding him. Counted minutes gathered the five friends before their final parting. Because of that, Speax turned to Paulo, intentionally in the terrestrial's language with his dissociable manner of speaking.

"Well, the long-awaited moment is coming, Paulo. In a very few minutes we'll part for a long time. If you want, it won't be forever."

"We'll come back again. We promise you," Pat chimed in, too.

"And you bestir closely among the people. Unstick them a bit from things," Khoren added.

"And look for the Man! Even with a lantern!" concluded Mot.

"But don't shine the lantern against the Sun!" was Speax's last bit of advice. "That's it. The experiment is over. Look, the Earth!"

From the front, the blue disc of the native planet quickly enlarged. A dense diaper of clouds covered a considerable part of it. White spiral whirls swam in the atmosphere. The continents became more and more distinctly visible. The azure was coming increasingly closer, while the disc took up the whole space before their eyes. The "flying saucer" had lightly made its way into the atmosphere and headed for South America.

However, when penetrating the atmospheric layers, Paulo began to run up against the surprises given by Earth. It was not quite the same. Along with the feel of the thrill and agitation of returning to hearth and home, he could not fail to notice all the novelties around him. His heart fluttered with joy while his mind impressed the changes. And they were not few; they commenced still by the space. It had been settled by numerous satellites, much smaller in size than the former ones, as well as new laboratories and stations. As he understood later, not all of the orbital complexes had scientific purposes. Some of them were in the tourist business—they were hotels and camping sites. However, others were weapons—heavy laser guns oriented towards Earth. And some of it was just space junk, so much space junk waiting for someone to clean it at last!

Descending more and more, Paulo guessed that the atmosphere was much clearer than before—there did not seem to be smog above the cities. He wondered whether the ozone holes had disappeared. Oh, yes—they had shrunk, and there was no trace of them.

Paulo didn't notice at all when he set foot on the ground. Everything happened so quickly that he still couldn't collect himself. And suddenly he felt the parting. Speax stood beside the capsule, silent and serious. Paulo became aware that his throat had dried up, that something strangled him. He did not expect such a response from himself at all. He thought that all would be ended by a handshake only. But suddenly, something welled up inside him and shook him up with all its might. Something overturned in his soul, as occurs when true friends bid farewell—almost as a physical pain as if tearing something off from yourself. Why had this distant, in every respect human stood so well with him?

There were no hugs; there was not even a handshake. All happened without any display of feelings.

"Farewell, my friend," the extraterrestrial said, raising his arm.

"Farewell, Speax!" screamed the youth.

The "flying saucer" abruptly left the ground, and in a jiff disappeared into space.

Feeling his feet, Paulo looked all around where he had been left alone. He was located on the same spot where he had been kidnapped. The coppice and river were the same. The space traveler went to the bank and sat down for a while along it. A light breeze whiffed by. He stared at the river. How much water had flown down it since then? All seemed to him only a dream, a nice dream, short and enthralling. As if he had dreamt with his eyes open. And now all at once it was over. Would he be put under stress again? Would he fall again into some unknown world? Thirty-four whole years had passed, which probably had changed Earth much more than the last three-hundred-forty.

Paulo began to pace slowly towards his home. He wanted to breathe in deeply the familiar air. He wanted to tread along with his memories, which walked together with him as if alive.

However, after a while, when he left the coppice behind, he noticed that the one-time bare meadows of wanton plays were missing. They had turned into vast plantations divided into plots. Paulo did not know that these were plantations for fast-growing trees requisite for the extraction of bio-gas, which served as an energy source. He tried to guess at their type and sort, but alas, unsuccessfully, because these saplings were unknown to him.

The way led him to the old footbridge where the river curved its wet back. How many times, when they were children, had he jumped with Manuel into the water from it?! How many times had impish voices and water splashes merged here in joint rapture—cheery and with sheer joy?! But now the relic was missing. There was a pretty, elegant bridge made of light and strong composite materials that had replaced the old one at the same spot.

Here is the home! The native home! To return under the paternal roof! The thrill is unique!

It was on the same spot, but it was not the same house. It was bigger, in a broken line with two wings. There were beautiful stairs—a splendid front staircase and a winding one at the right wing. In front of the home was a well cropped lawn and nice park creating enjoyable freshness. Paulo began to wonder if he had landed in some other place. No, he had landed in some other time.

The young man began to become afraid about whether he would even recognize his own parents, if at every step all things were so changed. Therefore, with some uncertainty, he rang the bell.

An elderly woman of about seventy-five years old came out. She was, in appearance, a well-preserved old lady, but with tired and sad eyes. She was his mother. After a moment of stupor, she recognized her son.

"Paulo, my child!" Trembling all over, the old lady stood as if nailed to the ground. "Are you, my boy? Oh, my God, I can't believe it! This is not possible!" She stepped back in a fit of light-headed dizziness.

Paulo rushed forward and embraced his mother. He took her hands and began to kiss them.

"I am, Mum, I am. Don't you see?"

"There is a God in the heavens, I was sure! My Paulo! You left looking the same, quite the same, so many years ago! Good Lord, I'm probably dreaming! But, how do you disappear suddenly, and, later on, after a coon's age, suddenly appear again, the same boy as you have always been, as if just now you came back from the University? We had already buried you, my boy. Speak. Tell me all … all about your missing time. Come on, talk. Talk! What happened to you? Where were you until now, all this long time?"

"In the hereafter, Mum," Paulo said, smiling.

"Don't joke with your old mother! But it seems that it is so, since you arose and stand before my eyes. Tell me, yet don't joke, because it comes to me in excess."

"I do not joke. Not in the least. Did Manuel say nothing to you?"

"He mentioned, of course, about some "flying saucer," but I didn't believe him. I took it all for a sheer cock-and-bull story. I thought there had been some crime, which he concealed for reasons unclear to me. But I couldn't imagine that he was connected with it. I just didn't know what to think. But … let's go in. How slow I am! Forgive your old mother. We stand at the door, but it didn't come to my mind to invite you in."

The two went inside the house. It belonged, obviously, to a well-to-do family, who could afford such a good interior. But there was next to nothing in it to preserve his child-hood memories, except some old furniture, maybe. His mother had kept some old household goods as cherished relics.

"But why don't I see anyone? Where are the others? Where's Daddy? Silvia?"

"Your father is dead, Paulo."

"Dead? When? What was the reason? Why is he dead?" Paulo opened his eyes wide, startled by the unexpected sad piece of news, the surprise in succession in his home nest.

"He died of a heart attack ten years ago. He worked hard and sorely overtired himself. And the result was not long in coming. One day I found him slouching on the writing-desk in his study. His heart couldn't bear it. I felt it keenly when he left me, too."

"And now you're living alone?"

"No, your sister Silvia got married, and since your father's death, the three of us live here now, together with the children. A couple of days ago they went to Europe for three months. Joao, her husband, flies there often on business, and this time he took them all along with him."

"What about Manuel? What happened to him?"

"Manuel became a famous mathematician. After he finished his studies here, he continued his education in the United States. And then he moved there. They say he's one of the greatest authorities on computers. Your cousin holds a professorship in Princeton, but now they've drawn him in the Second moon base program, which should be completed soon, and because of that, he's lived with his family in Houston for the past two years."

Paulo went near to his mother and clasped her to his breast with fondness. Afterwards, he kissed her filially. The family reunion was so unusual and so touching that mother and son had forgotten everything around them. But while the son was the same age as she had known him, the mother was obviously aged. Her silver hair, however, only intensified her carriage of a deserving matron.

Paulo told his mother the whole story in minute detail. She listened to his words closely and could not believe all of this. It sounded to her like a fairy-tale by Charles Perrault or Hans Christian Andersen, such as she once was fond of telling him when he was a child. Now it seemed to her that the roles were changed. The chat went on until late into the night, while the feelings were calmed down a little, the violent emotions allayed.

15

He looked at himself for a while in the mirror. It was the same black hair, the same blue eyes, a fair complexion, and a beautiful small beard with a dimple on it—features that had been left in everyone's memory here before his flying away to *there*. He looked at himself in full height—a thin, slender, well-built young man. No, he hadn't changed.

However, so many things here had changed. Except for his mother's old furniture in the room downstairs, all the rest was different and new—even this bathroom. A computer was everywhere and in everything. It was just another family member.

Paulo decided to take a bath. With his hand, he tested the water in the tub. It seemed cool to him. Dissatisfied, he muttered out loud, "Warmer!"

The computer dutifully carried out his wish. However, the water still appeared cool to him, so he ordered a second time, "I said, you—warmer!"

Now he could enter the water. He took off the wrapper and dipped into it. He relaxed. Not only the water, but the tub predisposed to this, too. It was not the old metal tub. It had nothing in common at all with any traditional, stiff tub; rather, it was ductile like rubber, with a pleasant configuration and caramel-colored. It was comfortable and warm insulating. This tub was made of three layers of material. The substratum, for stiffness, was made of fiber-glass; the middle layer, supplying nearly all the thickness, was special polyurethane foam; while the upper layer was only a strip of elastomer polymer. In this tub, if someone slipped, he could not break his head when he fell. In fact, he could not slip at all.

After an exceptionally pleasant, relaxing bath, Paulo climbed out of the water.

"Robe and towels lie in the big wing of the locker, sir," explained the computer.

"The locker?" Paulo mimicked it. "Oh, yes."

He slipped the garment on, and, at this moment, heard behind him again the familiar metal voice, "Have a nice day, sir."

"Oh, I'm touched, wise guy."

The lad came out of the bathroom, and, as he had on a robe, went to the kitchen and looked for something to drink. He opened the fridge and hunted for a beer. But he already knew that, besides the speaking bathrooms, there existed also speaking fridges that explained their inner state and control system, as well as their correct usage.

Opening the door of this appliance was as if he had opened its mouth. "Sir, I have in myself sweets on the second rack, four pounds of chicken meat and four pounds of pork in the locker, and five packets of butter and twenty eggs in their special containers—"

"Okay, okay, where's the beer, know-it-all?" Paulo broke in with annoyance, searching for the beverage. After he found the cooling drink, he opened the can and began to drink thirstily.

"Sir, for correct service use, you must not leave me open for more than twenty-five seconds. Close my door, please."

"Well, dear, you're so open anyway! One can't take the words out of you!"

The young man closed the fridge and mumbled under his breath, "The hell with it. Back *there* no one uttered a word to me, no one talked to me, but here all I get is talking, at every step chatty chests!"

Paulo went to his room to dress. He looked at his clothes. Before alighting from the starship, they had given him back his old clothes and took back the red costume. He drank a draught from the beer. *I'll keep these rags as a museum exhibit*, the youth thought it over. *Though, they're a peerless keepsake.*

Compared with them, his new clothes, which he bought the previous day, were genuine Sunday clothing. They were beautiful, convenient, smart, functional, and, most important, they were climatic. The socks that he pulled on, the pants and the T-shirt that he put on, though parti-colored, all were made of the same stuff, impregnate with polythene-glycol. These clothes warmed in cool weather and cooled in warm weather. They did not crease and were hardly ever soiled. They were excellent in every respect. In fact, the carpet on which he had stepped was also woven of this practical stuff.

When he was ready, Paulo hurried outdoors. He considered taking a stroll. His nose constantly caught a pleasant aroma. All around him floated the fresh fragrance of pine, and he breathed it in gladly. These clothes were made that same way—wafting of a lasting aroma of flowers, herbs, or trees, according to the personal taste of the client.

He was off to the park. He walked slowly and absently. The memories rushed into his head, one after the other. It was as if yesterday. His daddy carried him in his arms, ran with him; they scuffled... His daddy!...But now he was not here. Paulo did not even get to see him grow old. Just here was where daddy took pictures of all three of them. And here, on this bench, Paulo was fond of sitting down to read. To read! Oh, yes, he had to resume his university studies or, to be precise, to begin them all over again. But how would he be perceived by the others? His troubles would probably begin in the passport-issuing office when he goes to renew his identification papers. They will ply him with questions about anything and everything. Even his mother could hardly help him as a witness. What else, however, could be done? It is not possible to live in anonymity.

The cosmic pioneer decided to return and set off back down the alley. In front of his eyes, like a ghost, Manuel appeared. He had been fond of sitting right here on the grass to solve his fluxional equations. Paulo had to see him; had to see him at any cost and as soon as possible. What was he doing, what was he concerned with now?

Before long, Paulo found himself in front of the house again. But he didn't want to go in. He stared at the house. It had been built with a new technology, as many others had similarly been. These were bio-homes—buildings and houses constructed of natural materials: clay, brick, wood. The plasterer's putty and the paints were completely innocuous and did not cause allergies. In these bio-homes there were built-in solar-system thermostats for regulating the internal temperature. Head colds and infections could barely be found in them. These bio-homes made up nearly fifty percent of all newly-constructed buildings, but in the rich countries only. Along with them, there were also houses constructed of plastic, with wiring, heating, ventilation, water pipes, and sewage-removal built into their walls. Really, they were ecological, cheap, and spacious enough, but some people preferred the others—just because they were cheap.

It still seemed to him too early to come back home, although the day was already declining. He advanced to the river. When he got ashore, spread out far and wide in front of his eyes were endless areas planted with different farming crops. Even the farming had become different during these thirty-four years. Electro-reclamation of the soil had been known for a long time, but now it continued to be applied even with more success. It had artificially produced highly productive earth. Man had created a soil with rare, earlier-unthinkable properties. Lavish irrigation was applied everywhere. Besides that, cobaltic water was poured on the farming crops as disinfection against vermin, as well as to give much higher yields. They had even created luminous tomatoes, which shone with a red light in the dark, and the salad from them was not only tasty but funny too. From the global computer network, Paulo learned later that, in the cold, sub-polar regions, large-scale conservatories with artificial heating and lighting, not only of the air but of the soil too, were used. Gene engineers had created valuable and hardy varieties under variable physical and chemical conditions. The pastoral farming of the old times gave way to the modern—marine, bacterial, micro-algae. What kind of sunflowers would Van Gogh paint now? But would he even paint sunflowers at all?

16

Paulo spent about a month at home. He decided, however, to visit his cousin Manuel in the United States. As he expected, there were problems in the passport-issuing office when he went to renew his identification papers. They looked at him like he was quite a character. If he had fallen from the Moon, they would more easily have believed him. But what else could he tell them but the truth? This, by the way, wasn't too far from the truth. Every other story would sound like a fish tale, and even more. If he told them that he had hibernated for the past thirty-four years and had just now awoken—what then? Or that he had been reincarnated? Would this be better? Scarcely.

Paulo entered the police station. The chief of the local police was sitting in his chair staring at his papers. He was approximately sixty years old, plump, and bald. He drank a cup of coffee. Just at this moment Paulo faced him.

"Sir, I have to tell you about an event of utmost importance."

"Oh, an event of utmost importance? Have, by any chance, extraterrestrials attacked us by surprise?"

"No, not quite … I have to renew my identification papers."

"And this is an event of prime importance? Your papers are an event of the utmost importance? Listen, lad, you're in the wrong room."

"No, no, sir. Hear me, please. I don't know where to begin. This is so strange, an improbable story... So, I was kidnapped by a UFO," Paulo shot out in the air.

"Yes, of course. As for me, I'm from Mars," the fatso caustically replied.

"I tell you this seriously, quite seriously."

"Oh, yes, yes. And how did this happen?"

Paulo began to explain. However, when he came to his settlement on Omeron, the sheriff jumped suddenly to his feet and called loudly into the next room, "Domingo, move your bottom and immediately fetch Dr. Almeida, the main doctor at Specialized Hospital for Mental Diseases, and bring him here. We have an emergency! And you, young man, will wait here for the doctor." He turned back to his desk. "Oh, my God, what a century we live in! Man becomes woman, woman becomes man, and just as we get used to this idea, now one more insane case. Abducted by aliens! Damn it! And all of them want new identification papers! My Lord! What else will happen to me? I have to retire on a pension. What haven't I seen until now, but this comes to me in excess," the policeman concluded his tirade.

After nearly half an hour, Dr. Almeida's medical team was in the police office. Meanwhile, Paulo rang his mother and told her that he had problems getting the documents. She came quickly and confirmed her son's words. Then the cop got a shock.

"Doctor … Felipe," the officer began slowly, "you have a patient. Or, maybe two—mother and son. Either I'm going mad, Doctor, or they're both crazy. They assert the same thing, that the youngster was kidnapped by aliens, but then they returned and brought him back. And I don't care a fig about them, but they want me to issue new identity papers. The young man is twenty-four years old, but he ought to be fifty-four, according to his birth certificate. So, I need your assistance, Doctor."

In a couple of days, Dr. Almeida gave his answer. "Look, Gustavo, we're known each other for many years. I've dealt with all kinds of unhinged people, but such a case I've never had. We ran all the compulsory analyses and tests on them. We twice subjected them to interrogation by polygraph. They were even in a state of hypnosis, and I can tell you—they're completely normal. We have only one course left—the only possibility to accept as real is that the events they relate are actual facts and that they lived through them as they described. That's it. By the way, in the UFO Society, there are so many such cases described. It's just the first time I'm personally facing this problem."

So, finally, Paulo got his documents. And immediately set out for the United States. He decided to acquaint himself with all the technical miracles of the epoch by entering into direct contact with them. For this reason, he planned not to take a usual passenger plane to the States, but a space one. However, at the present, such a plane was flying only in São Paulo and Rio in Brazil. There was a project to soon open a new line to the capital city of Brasília.

So, Paulo had to take the train to Rio. However, this train had nothing in common with the trains from the second half of the twentieth century. Now the train was a real luxury. In competition with common air transport, the rail had already won, if not the contest, at least an appreciable advantage reclaiming the position it gave away thirty years ago. The train had become highly attractive. With its rather lower ticket price, the rail transport offered much more conveniences at the same traveling time. The train-eel was a kind of magnetic levitation vehicle that gathered speed up to three hundred and ten miles per hour. Besides that, the compartments were no longer small spaces for many people, but more like hotel rooms. It was a cheap *Orient Express* for the middle-class citizen. Each compartment was fitted out with all the modern conveniences—a completely furnished, comfortable room with a TV set, cell phone, radio, bathtub, and toilet. There was a dining car, a bar car, and a business lounge car. It had all been made for pleasant and comfortable traveling. So, the train had its advantages—speed close or equal to a plane's, but at the same time offering individual restful conditions, as well as the fact that the separate motor carriages left every thirty minutes, one after another, and in this manner they could convey a great number of passengers. This was not the old train of 1989 conditions, but a traveling hotel, even a "flying hotel." This train was a product of the unmanned technologies and was full automated and self-monitored, i.e., traveling without human conductors and ticket-takers, but by computer alone.

Tickets were not sold in stations and, because of that, ticket offices were missing here. Tickets were sold to every passenger in advance online through the world computer net or in the compartment by the computer accepting the traveler's credit card. Then it produced in seconds on the spot, which instantly calculated the ticket price according to the distance, and gave it up in a trice.

Paulo boarded at the last door at the end of the train and rented a room. In a little more than two hours he would be in Rio. How the world had shrunk. In the previous *modern* railroad, he had traveled more than ten hours to reach that destination!

The compartment computer was very courteous and explained everything in the room to him, and then left him in private with a wish for nice traveling. Paulo sat down in the chair and stared out through the window. On the platform, as always, many people in a hurry passed by—travelers departing and persons accompanying them, and travelers arriving and persons welcoming them.

After a while, when the train moved off and quickly gathered speed, and when nothing could be distinguished outside yet, the window suddenly became a picture. It was a marvelous seascape, with the sun in a blue sky, and it looked quite genuine. This was an electronic window, as the computer explained. According to the traveler's wish, the picture could be changed or it could change by itself during the trip in a manner that made an illusion of movement. For example, if at departure from the initial station the scenery was of a sunrise, in the terminal station it would be sunset already, while if it was a sunset at the beginning, it could turn into a full-moon night in the end.

Really, thought the young man, *this is all very nice. But it's all made for the secluded man or maybe for the lonely man out of touch with the world, out of touch with others, such as he emerges to be soon. The old compartments were more cramped, but weren't they more fun and interesting?*

He took the phone and ordered a ticket for the liner after his connection to the Rio airport. He had failed to do this at home. His order was immediately carried out. After that, the traveler sat down on the bed and switched the TV set on. On a music channel, a nice tune was playing in video clip, the latest hit on the world charts. Humming, he fell on his back on the bed with wide open arms. He went to sleep faintly smiling. In this way, he did not even feel when they arrived.

Since his time was mapped out, he took a taxi to the airport. Paulo noticed at once that this car was exceptionally streamlined, much more attractive, with much better and more functional design than the smartest sports cars of before. Automation was everywhere inside. It could function without a driver. The car could cope with all tasks quite alone. In fact, there already were such tentative taxis in the vehicular traffic—the driver was the on-board computer. If he wished, the client himself could even be the taxi driver. Not only unlocking and locking the car doors, but starting the engine also happened with the client's credit card, thereby making the payment automatic from the time the car started, the distance covered, to switching the engine off.

Paulo did not wish to be a driver and sat down on the other seat. He only poked his credit card where required, and the car started on its own. It stopped on its own at the crossings where the traffic lights were red and drove off on its own when they turned green. This car could always prevent an accident with the car in front of it by abruptly stopping, if this was needed. It chose the optimum route to the airport and let its traveler off there on time.

Paulo alighted from the taxi and headed towards the spacious edifices of the air-complex. Since the space-plane used the same runways for taking off and landing as the common planes, the airfield complex had been so expanded that it was impossible to use the traditional gate layout. For this reason, a little subway on magnetic levitation had been built, which transported the travelers quickly, comfortably, and safely.

At the passport control spot, a slender blonde woman with blue eyes stood—a sexy young girl with a charming smile, voluptuous bosom, and a sweet-voice like a nightingale. She was extremely surprised when she compared the personal information on Paulo's passport with his appearance.

"But you … you are fifty-four?"

"No, young lady, I'm twenty-four; at that—not full age. Doesn't it show me?"

"Yes, I see your point, sir," she replied, looking at the passport again, quite perplexed, but then changed to suspicion. "But then your passport is forged."

"No, young lady, it's genuine, too. According to it, I could be your father. But according to me, I could be your lover."

"It's better you stay on the spot and wait for a minute."

The girl called in the border officer on duty and explained the incident to him. He took the passport and went into his office again. Using his computer, the officer immediately made contact with the police station in Paulo's native town. After the relevant checkup in his personal file, the border officer came back.

"Everything is okay, sir. Excuse us for the trouble. I'm sorry. Please, do enter the departure hall."

Paulo turned around and winked at the beautiful blonde. She requited him with an impish smile and such a wink, too. Not expecting such a response, he laughed and entered the departure hall while waving goodbye to her.

The hall was large and light. The travelers were seated in soft armchairs, in expectation of the call for boarding the plane. The enormous metal bird was seen through the window panes as if it was thrilling and with an impatient impulse to fly. The military version of this hypersonic plane was a super powerful bomber, but its civil version was called *West Express*. This model was made in the United States. It took off and landed by normal tracks, while another model of a space plane was projected to take off from the rear of another usual passenger airplane. Americans began the tests of this last word in aviation technologies in 1993, while the first flight was implemented in 2019, so it had already performed flights for four years. Because of the constantly increasing stream of travelers, American companies had positioned themselves most quickly to the most efficient usage. The concentration of big masses of people in the cities suggested handsome profits. Especially in East Asia, where there was a large, concentrated urbanized center with sixty million travelers per year. The space plane, flying nearly seven thousand miles in two or three hours, kept direct connection and quick transport between Asia, Europe, America, Africa, and also Australia, that distance being 7,270 miles. The "flea's leap," as they jocularly called this flight, was realized by a velocity twelve times higher than the speed of sound, at nearly thirty miles in altitude.

The travelers were called to board the plane. The airport's subway conveyed them to it. Here, seen at close quarters, it looked still more imposing and mighty. A moving staircase carried the people upwards into the plane.

Paulo found his seat by the hatchway and sat down. People of different nationalities also took their seats. Presently they heard the soft and pleasant voice of the stewardess.

"Dear travelers, welcome aboard space plane *West Express* with Captain Richard Jackson. We'll fly at an altitude of twenty-eight-and-a-half miles at a velocity of just over two miles per second. Tighten your seatbelts, please. Thank you. The crew of *West Express* wishes you a nice trip."

The motors had already started and now they began to work at higher revs. The plane slowly moved off and taxied to the runway for takeoff. When it got there, it stopped in start fever. After a surge of power, the bird rushed forward, in crazy running on the concrete path. Hundreds of thousands of horse-power harnessed together, rushed into impetuous racing, which pressed all the travelers close to the chairs. Before long, the cosmo-plane suddenly broke away from the runway, and Paulo felt the familiar contraction in his stomach, which, strangely, was missing in the Omeronean space capsules.

The cosmic sight was not new for him to be impressed. Moreover, it was not even really cosmic. So, Paulo waited and easily ate the snack that an attractive stewardess served him. Through the hatchway, however, he delighted in a beautiful sight—Earth shining like a neon pearl on the border of its atmosphere, with the black darkness of infinite space behind. What irresistible charm emanated from this blue crystal sphere! He saw again the scattered satellites flying around.

The trip lasted an hour or so.

Houston was affable. It met its guest with warm and sunny weather. Paulo took a taxi again, which led him to the accurate address.

The car stopped in front of a magnificent two-storied house with a little garden outside it. The young man stepped onto the walkway leading up to the house. The sweeps of grass were carefully kept, which, together with the flower-beds in front of the house, where exquisite tulips bloomed in different colors, formed a trim garden. About ten steps from the tulips, symmetrically placed on both sides of the house, rose shrubs stuck up. By the side of one of them—the one on the left—was a sculpture, a perfect replica of Auguste Rodin's *The Thinker*.

Well, well, Manuel, Paulo thought for a while. *Manuel the thinker!*

He pressed the button next to the door. As a result, he heard on the interphone the voice of the home computer. "Family Roberto is away from the home. Please leave your name and phone number, as well as a message, if you consider that necessary."

Paulo looked round about. Suddenly, he noticed perched up on the right, a little like a lady-bird, a video camera. His presence was already documented on a recording, too. After coming home from the office, Manuel would be able to see all the people who had looked for him during the day. However, there was still a lot of time until the evening. It was obvious that Paulo had not picked a suitable time. It was a good thing that he had the address of Manuel's office, too.

He took a taxi again, which led him away to the institute. It was a very tall building made of aluminum and glass. The elevator, extraneous and vitreous, hauled him up to the seventh floor, where he had to find his cousin. After asking for him, a man in white overalls pointed a finger at the office.

The youth knocked and entered. A man with lightly ash-colored hair was on a video conference call with his partners. He was sitting on a comfortable swivel chair, with his back to the visitor. He failed to notice the entering of an alien person.

For this reason, after he switched the connection off, the man jumped up out of his chair and, at a quick pace, was off to leave the room. And only just at this moment did he see that there was a man in the room. He stopped. He started to ask "Who are you and what do you want?" when he stopped, startled, and blinked his eyes two or three times. *Is this him or not?* he thought.

"Manuel, do you not recognize me?" In this instant, his cousin broke the brief silence. "I am Paulo."

"Good God! Paulo? It can't be! No, the hell with it! This is impossible! Are you real? Let me touch you."

Manuel came near to Paulo, touched him, joggled him, pinched himself, and went on to doubt his own eyes. There were so many frauds, real and virtual, in the world.

"Well, no! If miracles don't occur, then what are you? This is a subject even mathematics cannot prove! No, no, this is bad joke. Maybe a hallucination? Actually, I overtire myself so much lately. I'm working so hard." Manuel was highly excited by the swift meeting.

He set out for the door. But close to it he stopped, turned around, and looked back. Paulo stood in the middle of the room as before and was smiling. Manuel came back and ran his fingers over Paulo again.

"Okay, boy, you're his double and a dexterous swindler. You've learned everything about my cousin and now you'll blackmail me, is that so? Well, what do you want? Want me to call the guards?"

"Enough, Manuel! That's going too far."

"But what is all of this then?"

"Paradox of the twins, Manuel. And if you want, paradox of the cousins is better. Did you forget what happened to us?"

"Just because I haven't forgotten it, doesn't mean I thought I'd ever see you again. There is no such case. No one has ever come back from the next world, much less someone kidnapped by a UFO!"

"These words I already heard in the police office. But, in fact, there is a man—Ezekiel—who, the Bible says, was kidnapped by a UFO and then sent back home."

"But then you have to explain everything to me. Everything!"

"Here and now?"

"Of course not. Wait for a minute."

Manuel took his mobile phone out from the inside pocket of his jacket. The smart phone was rolled up, and, in order to use it, Manuel unrolled it. The amazing thing was that the display's dimensions were larger than the smart phone itself. Manuel dialed the code for his home and ordered the home computer to fill the bath-tub, prepare the dinner, and to switch on the musical system with nice music in fifteen minutes when they would be home. After that, he connected to the automated underground garage and ordered the computer-dispatcher to have his car waiting for him at the entrance in front of the Institute.

"I ordered the dinner by the computer because it's possible my wife will be late. Her team is making laboratory tests with base biological crops, and because of that she usually returns late in the evening. We'll just have more time to have a private chat. That's, of course, if the daughters leave us alone. Let's go."

The both came out and set off for the elevator. They resembled father and son.

17

Nobody was at home yet. It was locked. But instead of looking for the key, Manuel shouted, "Open Sesame!"

And the door opened by itself. Just like in the fairy tale. The computer unerringly discerned the voice of the home's proprietor and opened the door to him only. His wife and children were the only others that could enter this way. Nobody else. Obviously, the computer had already mastered everything everywhere.

They entered. Music wafted inside. From somewhere, with perfect crystal purity, Vivaldi was heard. They were the undying chords of the "Spring" concerto from *The Four Seasons* series.

"Take your seat, Paulo," Manuel suggested, offering him a chair. "I shan't be a minute. And what'll you take to drink?"

"Whatever you're having. I hope that, at least, you're drinking whisky without a computer's assistance. The endeavor is worth it, isn't it?"

"Do you know that you're right? Only jeans and whisky have stayed the same as they were. Only they have unchanged from their first day. More ice?"

"Yes, if you please."

Presently, the host came back with two glasses and sat down in the armchair next to his *extraterrestrial* guest.

"Cheers! For this unthinkable get-together!"

"Cheers!" answered Paulo.

After the glasses jingled, Manuel took a sip and began. "All I remember from that day is that a flying saucer landed not far from us where we were angling in the river. I remember that suddenly, no one knows how, we found ourselves inside it. Those guys hypnotized us as if by their eyes. They gave us something to drink, and after that I woke up more than three hundred miles from home. All of this struck a mystery in my mind, and I always wondered whether it really happened—was it true, or wasn't it? Only your disappearance convinced me that this was not a dream but a sheer reality. Actually, what precisely happened then?"

"All of what I tell you will appear fantastic to you. I'm afraid all of this will sound like a fable to you, but it is the very reality, because, as you see, I myself have come from there. This is a wholly other world, Manuel. And we, our civilization, are the spit and image of it but in embryonic form, and not only us. You know that by using a DNA matrix, it is possible to be made and spread countless copies of RNA. By such a social matrix, copies of civilizations of human societies, among them ours, are made and spread, at least in the Near Space. Do you know that all our myths and legends turn out to be true? Do you know that all religions are filled, not so much with mysticism, as with truth? And I think within myself that, if Christ came to Earth, he came from there. He was one of them!"

"Wait, wait! Wait a minute." Manuel lifted his palm to stop Paulo. "What are you talking about? What does that mean? You quite confuse me. Where is this *there*?"

"They call it Omeron, but for us this is the star 61 in the Cygnus constellation."

"Cygnus constellation? It is the sacred constellation of many peoples in antiquity, not just the Hellenes."

"Yes, you know perfectly well the basic configuration of this constellation—a cross. It's a nice, regular, enormous cross—the symbol of Christianity. It has remained a symbol, not so much because Christ was nailed on it, but to show where he was sent from. I think so anyway. For they all were like him there. They all led life as this religion professes. Everyone was a god. Just like him. A hundred billion people! Can you imagine? This is a world of non-violence. There are no poor there, because there are no riches. Money does not exist there, nor any of our Earthly sins."

"They have no money? How's that?"

"They've had it. But now they don't. A long time ago they overcame that, as well as the State."

Paulo narrated everything to him during the next two hours. His cousin wondered so much about all of this. Even his logical mind could not imagine such a social system. Finally, the topic of the conversation switched to Manuel's work. He, on his part, acquainted his guest with mankind's development on Earth during these past thirty-four years. The staple of his narrative was the space programs, in the last of which he now participated also.

"Our energies until now were directed mainly to mastering two planets—the Moon and Mars. On the Moon, we have already built our base, which will serve as a way-station for the other planets, mostly for Mars. For its construction, technologies were developed for the production of moon concrete. The components of this concrete—sand, cement, and water—which are used to build the moon boroughs, are mined on the Moon itself. The hardest task was to discover water in the moon soil. Searching for ice, searching for frozen water in the moon craters, was assignment number one, as it was especially needed for the daily wants—for maintaining the vital conditions, as well as industrial needs—as a source of oxygen for the plants and of hydrogen for rocket fuel. For that reason, from the very beginning, we sent highly skilled specialists for construction of the moon base, which initially had temporary buildings only, protected against adverse outside factors. It was both dwelling-place and working place at the same time."

Manuel stood up with his whisky in hand and walked slowly to the windows. Paulo only now took heed of the room more precisely. The windows were unusual. Their glass generated energy and heat when it was necessary, while the beauty and coziness in this part of the room was created by the wallpapers, each of which shined in its own color. The host resumed his story.

"The beginning of the moon colonization was initiated in 2019. The Chinese were the first. They got ahead of all. Still, in December the previous year, they launched to the Moon their probe Chang'e-4 and almost on New year first day itself achieved a full success. For the first time a spacecraft from Earth touched down on the dark side of the Moon! The Chinese scientists sent there a container with seeds of cotton, soil with potatoes, yeasts and eggs of Drosophila melanogaster in order to explore whether they will be able to develop on the Moon in a closed bio-system. At first, the seeds germinated, but, unfortunately, immediately after that they perished under that benumbing cold there. However, this challenge was an enormous stride forward."

Manuel took a sip of whisky, smiled, and continued. "NASA reacted to this as if had stung. The Agency repeated the Chinese success a half year later. It began to cultivate vegetables and herbs on the Moon, with the single aim being to understand whether people could live there. Seeds for sowing were sealed up in tins containing all the seedlings needed to thrive. After landing, a trigger released a little reservoir with water in every tin, and a team on Earth watched how the seeds germinated when they were exposed to the moon's gravitation and radiation. In the same 2019, a sounding balloon was sent for topographic research of the Moon's surface in order to decide where exactly to place the First permanent base. The sounding balloon was put into polar orbit, and it provided us with sufficient information by which we could decide where to dispose our equipment. On the opposite, dark side of the Moon, we built an astronomical observatory with an enormous radio-telescope, which was completed in 2021. It is an ideal place there for astronomical observations, because of the lack of radio interferences and tremors. After all initial preparations and research, the inhabitation and the regular work in the base started in 2022, the last year, with extraction of ores and minerals. Now it is continuously improving prospecting and extractive engineering for gathering valuable metals and minerals that are requisite for future expeditions to the other planets."

"From the very beginning, the mastery of space was in cruel competition with the Russians. Where are they now?"

"The Russian penetration on the Moon? As you know, in the past, in contrast to us, the Russians started the exploration of the moon ground and relief with automatic devices instead of men.

But the dissolution of the Soviet Union, which occurred only two years after your disappearing, did not teach the Russian rulers to stake on the productive economy but not on its militarization. Their economy sank into deep recession because of technological backwardness and military expenditures. So, because of economic reasons, for want of funds, the Russians froze their exploration work on the cosmos. And here appeared the Chinese. For a short time, they amassed thorough knowledge and experience, which they used successfully. With the assistance of robots they located the spot for construction of their intended station. It was a compound made of three modules, which were assembled in Earth's orbit and then automatically directed to the Moon. Every station's module serves as a dwelling and, along with this, as a workplace for three cosmonauts. The robots built all the indispensable systems of living and work for them—electric power stations, plants for production of water and oxygen, as well as all the rest. Only when everything was ready for use—also in the last year of 2022—were the first Chinese settled.

The purpose of our Second moon base is to create a veritable Earth oasis among the wilderness there. We plan to gradually create a new kind of borough on the Moon, which will be able to provide man's natural living conditions. This reserve under its bell-glass will be an Earth in miniature. After its tests in the 90s in the last century in the program known as *Biosphere 2*, we decided that such modules could be created both on the Moon and Mars. And subsequently perhaps we'll do this on every new colonized planet."

"I know about the closed-system experiment of *Biosphere 2* as an idea. It was still only a forecast before I flew off from here. It involved a full circumrotation of the reserve's inner environment in pavilions with different climatic zones. In the Arizona desert, out of touch with the rest of the world, four men and four women had to spend a long time together among artificial streams and waterfalls, among different vegetation and living beings. Is that true?"

"Yes, this was the first mission. There was a second, too. The analysis of their scientific results, personal problems, and clashes was exceptionally valuable for science. And after the creation of the artificial soil, on this basis, it was inevitable we'd go on to create the program *Biosphere 3*. This program, our program, which was begun six years ago, is already at its end. All is created there. Only the settlers—plants, animals, and humans—are from Earth."

"Wonderful! Earth's humanity has advanced eminently in technical and technological respects. But how has it developed in social respects during these thirty-four years?" asked Paulo, thoughtful. "When I left Earth, it was shaken by social conflicts and wars. What's the situation now?"

"Now the situation in the world is worse than ever. Conflicts everywhere and of all kinds—stronger and more; conflicts of classes, races, religions, and migrants. The climate changed also—swelters and droughts alternate with floods and torrents; the winters are at times very open and without snow, at others severe and with snowdrifts. And the summers moved more and more to the north. There are no longer four seasons. Climate change and moral decline came true, exactly as according to biblical texts. It's as if mankind is near its end."

"This project—*Biosphere*—wasn't it designed, in fact, as a new Noah's Ark for saving Earth's life in case of an eventual global, social conflict and catastrophe?"

"Of course, there is that idea, too! As the last hope—"

"Hmm, the last hope … it's sadly …"

Rapt in the conversation, Paulo had not paid attention to the music playing, but now suddenly he lent his ear. It was *Moonlight Sonata*. He begged Manuel to turn up the volume. This was his favorite musical composition, and it served as a fine background to their conversation.

"Robbie, make the sound a little louder," Manuel shouted at the audio system.

And in a jiffy, the order was carried out, just as it should be.

"Do you know, Manuel, I'd like so much to hear *Moonlight Sonata* on the Moon. Will that ever be possible? It would be an exclusive experience."

"But this is not a problem. There are regular flights to the Moon. Tourist business has spread to the night luminary, too. For more than a year, every two weeks a transport craft carries curious passengers along with the catering for the base. And naturally, the rich. Since a ticket costs a hundred thousand dollars."

"A hundred thousand dollars? Ooh! I flew all the way to Omeron free of charge. One hundred thousand dollars for two hundred thousand miles, while for eleven light years—without money! You see the difference. A hundred thousand dollars! Indeed, only for the rich. If this is no problem –"

"But what are a hundred thousand dollars to a man with billions to fly to and walk on the Moon?"

"Excuse me, but I didn't know that you were a billionaire!"

"No, I'm not. I'm just a well-paid specialist. And because of that, I have no difficulty buying you a ticket. And I don't want you to feel obliged to me in any way."

"But what are you talking about? I cannot accept this gesture. This is really an alluring suggestion, but I cannot accept it. You do understand me, don't you?"

"Paulo, please do. I do this for the sake of our friendship. Besides that, it doesn't cost me so much."

"It costs you not so much?"

"Yes. My family has already been to the Moon on excursions twice. Unfortunately, I go there only on business." Manuel stood at once up and proposed, "I think we have to go into the kitchen to dine. You're surely belly-pinched. It's already half past seven."

The dinner was fish.

"My friend, the truth is that your home computer copes well," Paulo noted. "The taste of the fish is marvelous. How does this machine know to cook salmon?"

"It can do much trickier things than this. Cooking is its hobby."

"Oh, does it?" Paulo broke into a laugh. "Since it faultlessly gives advice for the wine's brand to accompany the fish, it surely is thus. And this music! It's as if it is an old connoisseur, both in music and the atmosphere for it."

At this moment the *Italian Capriccio* by Tchaikovsky was playing.

They were already eating fruit when they heard women's lively conversation and laughter approaching. These were Manuel's three women, i.e., his wife and two daughters. They were rather loud-mouthed.

"Three women in one place! You see what that means," Manuel rumbled out.

They laughed about something in the anteroom. It seemed they had begun to tell about various interesting experiences during the day while still standing in the doorway.

"As if all three of us had arranged to come home simultaneously," the voice of one of them was heard to say.

"Girls, girls, quiet," their mother said, trying to appease them. "Perhaps your father is tired if he's at home. Maybe he's still at work."

"Good evening, petticoat government," Manuel welcomed them when they appeared.

"Good evening, Dad," the daughters greeted him and rushed over to kiss him. Their mother followed suit.

"We have a dear guest. Please meet him. A messenger of another world, who, by mere chance, is found to be my cousin, too. This is Paulo. And these two are my daughters, Dolly and Sally. And my wife, Mary."

"I'm glad to meet you," Paulo said in his turn.

Mary was not very unlike her daughters. She looked rather like their elder sister. She was an attractive blonde of forty-two years with expressive blue eyes and looking slightly tired at this moment. Mary was the typical businesswoman—forward looking, devoted more to the job than to her home, stylish, and slender.

The two daughters looked very much like their mother, but with less similarity between them. Sally had auburn hair to her shoulders and was worn in a modish hairstyle, while Dolly possessed fair, curly, platinum hair almost to her waist. If Sally had in her blood the southern mettle of Manuel, Dolly couldn't be more different—she had an irresistible charm inherited from some northern race. She was a dazzling beauty with a sumptuous shape. Still then—upon their acquaintance—a mutual attraction flared up between her and Paulo, very deeply and hopelessly.

When he heard her name for the first time, Paulo ejaculated right off, "Dolly? Dolly Parton! But yes, quite the same! Don't you think? But at twenty years old."

"Who is she?" inquired Dolly.

"She doesn't know who Dolly Parton is?" Paulo addressed Manuel, surprised.

Later, when all present had learned the unusual fate of their guest, Dolly spontaneously proposed, "But this is a sensation! As early as tomorrow, we have to go on CBS or CNN! Or –"

"A sensation?" Paulo interrupted her. "On CBS? Just like in 1938? Like Orson Welles and his Martians? Come on, Dolly, you're not serious."

"But now it's not 1938! We're living a century later. Okay, then, maybe a news conference? But certainty we'll release an event on the Internet, on YouTube maybe, or on some other social networks –"

"Oh, no," Paulo was opposed. "Who'd believe all of this? Personally, I shouldn't like to become a TV or Web star."

"Indeed, now it's not 1938 when a mass of people believed Welles's radio drama about invading Martians, and he provoked a mass panic," remarked Manuel. "Now, on the contrary, nobody believes in anything."

"But … this is a unique event! It would be a crime if no one learns about this stupendous event!"

"Why? Do you think I'm the only such case? Perhaps there are lots of others. But mankind has been forced into accepting so many frauds as great truths that a small truth would sound to it like a great fraud."

"What about the rare chance for contact with another civilization?" the girl persisted.

"But I have no testimonies about that. Nothing. I don't carry any arguments, any proof. And it seems to me that we spoke too much about me. So, tell me now about you. I'd very much like to know what you are interested in, both professionally and in leisure."

It turned out to be a good, friendly conversation. Mary related with pleasure her experiments and her love of tennis. "I insist to emphasize," she said, "that in this home I have no adversaries on the court."

Dolly was a student of medicine, but in her spare time she very much liked to paint. And at that she was really talented. Her paintings were selling well. While Sally liked skiing and yachting too much. As a photo model, she used them both professionally and in leisure.

18

After two weeks' sojourn at his cousin's, the star wanderer quickly got used to his Earth life again, which promised him more and more of its delights and concerns, its plans and hopes.

Paulo sank more and more into his sleep, more and more he lost himself in its unknown expanses, when suddenly he felt the pleasant contact of a woman's nude, warm body. It was Dolly. Her hand lowered slowly and voluptuously from his chest to his abdomen and further down below.

"Dolly? You're crazy! What will your father say?!"

"My father can say nothing now."

"But this is incest. It's improper, do you understand?"

"It's not. Although I love him as much as a genuine father, he isn't my blood father."

"How's that?"

"Like that, he married my mother when I was almost two years old. I was born from her first marriage. Does that ease your mind?"

Her lips pressed on his, and only the night knows the further details.

Dawn had come long ago, but the wrestling had not yet calmed down. A prolonged moan was heard, a sensual sigh of satisfaction, and shortly afterwards, sitting in his lap, she sprawled on her back, exhausted with quickened pulse and breathing. The moment was dying down slowly, bit by bit. At this instant, as he was lying on his back, Paulo got up on his elbows, turned over on one side towards Dolly, and began to shower her body with kisses again.

"Oh, no! Enough!" Dolly opposed, pronouncing the words tiredly. "I can't anymore! I'm at the end of my tether. Eight hours of sex! Fantastic!" And she half-closed her eyes and shook her head with a smile full of satisfaction. "You're a real jewel, but I really can't take anymore! My legs tremble, and with this baseball bat," she indicated with a glance his male dignity, "you shattered me all over!"

"Why do you complain, I don't understand? Everything was just perfect!"

"Why? You ask me why? I can't sit down, I can't get up, I can't walk! I didn't know that you were that macho, darling. I was in need of eight hours sleep, not eight hours of sex!"

"But you were asking for it. Who's to blame, but you? Do you know that there aren't any women *there*?"

"Really? And you were left high and dry?"

"Thirty-four whole years!"

"What about men? Are they there?"

"There aren't."

"Oh, but this is awful! Are they epicenes?"

"They aren't. They're asexual. Higher and consummate beings. Angels. In the true sense of the word. They're another kind of people," Paulo replied to her quite seriously.

"As for me, I was jealous. Now I am even more."

"Of whom? Of them? You see, it's not worth it."

"No, of Dolly Parton. Who's she? You compared me with her from the first moment. When a man compares two women that means he has undoubtedly slept with at least one of them."

"Yes, in this instance with you. Not only the name, the bust, but even your dimples are the same as hers. At that time, she was a super show star in America, a singer, an actress, one of the most famous women in the world. I was a devout admirer, just like thousands of others. And she was, naturally, unattainable. But you see now she's in my hands. No, on my knees. I distrust my own eyes." Paulo began to laugh.

"But not the same one. How old is she now?"

"Now she should be eighty or more, I think. But when I saw her photos on the Internet, she seemed maybe twenty years younger. It's possible, as I learned at your place in the United States, middle age everywhere has risen to eighty-three years.

More than twenty percent of your population is over sixty-five. I don't know whether this is a nation aging or maybe rejuvenating. It seems Cindy Crawford's re-juvenescent sports programs really do work. By the way, do you know that your sister Sally looks like her?

"And who's *she*?"

"Another superstar and super beauty. She was mad about aerobics, as well as men about her."

"I see you've been a fan of many women in your time."

"The women in my time … Claudia Cardinale, Claudia Schiffer, Kim Basinger … The heavenly Kim! There's no such woman as she! And there won't be!"

"What do you say we go shopping?" Dolly said unexpectedly while getting up. Perhaps Paulo was not being tactful.

"Why not? A wonderful idea! We'll just take a little walk round the city."

"Button me up, if you please," begged the girl after handing him her brassiere. And it suddenly, like real, took the shape of her massive bust merely from the bodily warmth emanating from it because of the material it was made from—nitinol. This nickel-titanium alloy exhibited astonishing properties—shape memory effect and super elasticity. An online encyclopedia explained that "shape memory is the ability of nitinol to undergo deformation at one temperature, then recover its original, un-deformed shape upon heating above its 'transformation temperature.' Super elasticity occurs at a narrow temperature range just above its transformation temperature; in this case, no heating is necessary to cause the un-deformed shape to recover, and the material exhibits enormous elasticity, some ten to thirty times that of ordinary metal." So, even the underwear was touched by the new technologies!

After some preparation, mostly concerning Dolly's bathroom habits, the couple in love came out of the home. And it really was "in love." It had been two weeks already since the two lovers met, chatted, and flirted before this stunning night. It had been two weeks already in which they felt an overmastering desire each for other before this first *love night*. A mad night!

In fact, Paulo caught her every thought. Every look from her brought him information about her wishes and intentions, while she did not even suspect these abilities of his—or any other ones either, of course. But every man or woman in love is a bit of a telepathist. For Dolly also managed, to a certain extent, to understand his thoughts. Each impulse, each wail and gesture, each smile and look from one, were sucked in avidly with excitement and thrills by the other. It seemed, except the jeans and whisky, only love still remained the same. Who knows why, however, it did not encourage marriage. The more and more spreading form of living together was cohabitation. Lord Byron proved to be right that "there's doubtless something in domestic doings which forms in fact, true love's antithesis."

It's true that happy families are all alike. Well, after a divorce every family is unhappy in its own way. But in the very beginning all is exquisite—angels sing joyfully in chorus and sun shines and streams from everywhere. Being now in their pink space of time, Paulo and Dolly swam in bliss amongst the clouds.

They both set out along the alley for the car. Dolly was irresistible in her golden appearance.

"How many dresses like this do you have? I guess that the day before yesterday you wore something similar, but in azure, and before that, in some other color."

"It's the same dress. Only its color changes during every washing. I like it very much."

"Well, this is very frugal. You could go two years with just one dress."

"Well, well. I could do it for even five years. Thanks, but I wear it for a month only. After that, I give it away as an old belonging. Take this button and put it on your pants."

"But I close them by zipper, Dolly. And besides that, it works."

"This isn't a button for your fly, silly," she said, breaking into a laugh. "This is a micro-receiver. If you want, you can attach it to your shirt instead. With this device, you can know what is happening inside your home at any moment when you're away from it, thanks to the micro sender that is built in the interphone, giving signals for each noise."

"And yet, the crimes don't disappear, do they? They're only modified."

"Yes, indeed. The criminals adopt the new technical challenges and become more intelligent and more ingenious."

"But that's no way to behave! Going out on the street, one still has to beware of his kind!"

While opening her car door, Dolly replied, "That's so. But still, up to now no one has contrived a better social system, at least here in the United States." They sat down inside the car. "Look. These aren't usual earrings, they're electronic. So is this bracelet. A variety of electronic adornments for women are being produced like necklaces, brooches, and rings, and for children badges, even sheriffs, which are nothing but alarm systems of defense against theft, violence, or the like. In case of need, they immediately call the police."

"Why do you take them now? I'm with you."

"By habit, just in case. Oh, I've forgotten," she exclaimed and thrust her hand into her vanity-bag, took out a packet of pills, and swallowed one of them.

"Was that a birth control pill? Why don't you use better methods?"

"No," Dolly smiled, "this is a tanning pill. Instead of lying down under the sun or a quartz lamp, you can get a bronze tan after taking several such pills. I want a baby, darling," she volunteered, stretching over and kissing him.

"Aren't the pills dangerous? Don't they have any side effects?"

"No, they're completely harmless," replied the girl and started up the engine.

The healthy lifestyle had become a line of conduct for everyone who professed this new religion, and for that reason, he or she took all kinds of pills, sweated in the fitness hall, and ate wholesome food.

Inside the car, Paulo looked about. Even when he was traveling by taxi, he had paid no serious attention of the entire design of modern automobiles.

Outside, the car was perfectly streamlined, without handles and rear-view mirrors. For reverse eyesight, however, a video camera was mounted of the inside mirror's ex-place. The coupe was molded as a united whole with the frame by composite materials. The doors, only two, opened upwards like wings, not outward as by tradition. The engine performance, brakes, and gearbox were maintained in optimum order electronically by the onboard computer. In fact, since 1995, manufacturers had begun installing modern, shiftless transmissions for switching over with ease. The control appliances on the dashboard were seen as a projection on the windshield. In comparison with the cars of 1989, this was a fantastic technological leap into the future. The seats were immovably affixed to the floor, but in return the pedals were able to be moved back and forth according to the driver's height.

To a great extent, electric cars had the same construction. They were eco-friendly automobiles, and most of them used a variety of lithium-based batteries. The electric cars had a range of up to three-hundred-ten miles on one charge and a top speed of one-hundred-twenty-five miles per hour. The support infrastructure for all of this was quite good. For cars using batteries, everyplace from home to the mall had charging stations, while the cars running without a battery received their charge from electrified roads. In fact, the market was dominated by hybrid vehicles. For elimination of the noxious, especially toxic waste gasses, mostly under low velocities, in such cars electric motors were used at low speeds, while, to achieve high velocities, the internal-combustion engine kicked in, using hydrogen fuel, which was quite eco-friendly, too. Gasoline and diesel engines had already been forgotten and their vapors a wrongdoing.

During his final look around, Paulo noticed that above each door of the car, just above the travelers' heads, aside and upward, were two syringes. He asked, very perplexed, "Is this ambulance on duty? What are these syringes for? There aren't drug addicts among you, are there?"

"Don't worry. These are crucial injections. They contain a substance that strongly slows down the body's metabolism.

By one or two such injections, you can achieve a new, quite different metabolism. Since I majored in biology, I can explain it to you. This extract induces a body's retune-up on another, more frugal regime of metabolism. Under such a retune-up, a calibration of the neurochemical processes the metabolism slow considerably. Simply, the power consumption is redistributed among the various body's systems and tissues. In case of the animals, you know, hypobiosis exists as a winter sleep, as hibernation in bears, for example. Or think of the self-tune-up of the yogis, who achieve the same result when they lie buried sometimes even for a week on end, six feet underground. Under usual conditions, i.e., room temperature, the metabolism is slowed down seventy to eighty percent, while under a lower temperature, up to ninety or ninety-five percent. So, these injections are life-saving remedies."

These drastic remedies functioned immediately up to, at the latest, two or three hours. The controlled hypobiosis was a human's lifesaving practice. It was irreplaceable medical technology for extreme traumas: for instance, for sufferers from automobile accidents, from being buried underground in mining shafts or in destroyed buildings after earthquakes; in cases of famine or depletion of oxygen; in cases of lethal wounding; in cases of burns or of frost bites at the poles, in the ocean, or in space. In general, these injections were widely used in all kinds of extreme life-threatening conditions, in all kinds of risky professions. The purpose was, by one or two injections, for the metabolism to be practically stopped for whatever amount of time the sufferer needed to be taken off to the nearest hospital for professional medical aid and attendance. Each man, on his own, could give himself an injection under such circumstances. For that reason, the syringes were spread everywhere—in cars and trucks, in public transportation, in planes, in space and sea ships, and in homes and offices.

Paulo had already seen that the onboard computer could drive the car wholly by itself, could completely supersede the driver, and on account of that, two people could easily chat, as was the case now. For this purpose, the urban roads and crossings were equipped with sideways electronic sensors sending data about their condition under rain, fog, or slippery streets, as well as about crashes, heavy accidents, or traffic jams. All this information was collected in the central server which, on its part, spread it for all traffic. This information also was received by the onboard computer of each automobile and in this way it prevented its driver from unnecessary troubles or unforeseen incidents. The same applied to the highways out of cities, too.

An unconcealed interest for the star roamer was the electric car, which he was seeing shuttling everywhere. Many were combined with solar panels. They used solar energy, and only when it was impossible to do that did they turn on their own batteries. In some places, there were even roads and highways with wires buried beneath the asphalt, and the cars ran over them using electromagnetic induction. In crossing from one electrified section to another, they used their own batteries or the solar energy, which was caught by the photo cells mounted on the roof.

Such was the present. The automobiles' future, however, went beyond the bravest dreams! Owing to the nanotechnologies, the automobile of the near future would have be able to change its appearance on its own on molecular level as per the driver's wishing, as per the speed of wind; one appearance on the steep road upward and different downward; one appearance on a dirt road, and other on a high road. In a more distant future the car driving would have to be connected directly with the driver's brain and nervous system! Even the writers-fantast had no imagination for that!

The cars automatically stopped at crossings on the red signal. Paulo saw an innovation coming from Japan. These were the luminous pedestrian paths with changing colors—green, yellow, and red. The effect was thumping. The red path prevented absent-minded pedestrians from stepping into the road; but not the presuming ones, of course. Along with this, singing traffic lights were made for blind people: a nightingale's song warned them when they were coming to the crossing.

These clever traffic lights could let only ambulances pass automatically without hindrance at any time.

Everywhere, in every corner, vending machines were seen where one could buy beverages, cigarettes, sandwiches, and suchlike. But the young man was in need of performing another natural function, and with impatience cast his eyes about. At last, when he couldn't bear it any longer, Paulo asked Dolly where, in this big nice city, could one do a little odd job.

"Over there," she said, pointing at the facility, laughing.

One suddenly falling into the computer era would be very hard put to imagine its usage in such a simple place as the street toilet. The omnipresent computer! It was even here.

The street toilets, naturally paid, very much resembled the old telephone booths. But the *phone* now had another use. These were two joint cabins as neat as new pins. One of them exercised its direct official function, while the other sheltered the computer. It closely monitored whether all systems worked normally. In case of an irregularity, the computer notified the supporting office. For example, if the toilet paper was at the end of its roll, or if there was an intentional trespass. For serious damages, it closed the cabin until its repair by the technicians. Otherwise, during normal use, the door opened itself automatically after two or six minutes, as per the case.

After two minutes, obviously relieved, Paulo peeped outside. He came to the car's door, but didn't enter. Through the dropped glass, with the joy of an exempt captive, he addressed Dolly, pointing a finger at that place.

"Imagine what would happen if the computer didn't want to, forgot, or just failed to open the door. I'd be quiet inside at least a half an hour until the technicians arrived. And what if someone had to hold himself waiting for me?"

Dolly burst out laughing again. "Oh, no! You're the limit!" she almost cried.

Paulo did not get into the car. The street now represented unusual equipment, which made a great impression on him. Its sidewalks were movable! The pedestrians swept on top of them like jobs on a conveyor belt. Should they still be called pedestrians? Or, maybe, mobistrians?

Three-fourths of every sidewalk's width was taken up by these moving platforms, lying outside, while the resting fourth represented the traditional, ordinary urban sidewalk that led directly into the road. One treaded on a tile of the movable track and it bore him off ahead, at first with a slight acceleration, while eventually attaining the maximum velocity of twenty miles per hour. This was a horizontal elevator, a pedestrian conveyor that was compound by detached platforms. And when a man treaded on a tile, his platform quickened or slowed him separately from the other platforms, and thus he passed along with the rest of the traffic participations, i.e., pedestrians. The capacity of every conveyor was twelve thousand people per hour. Such separate *running* sidewalks were situated every one thousand, sixteen hundred, or thirty-two hundred feet, as well as between the crossings in the cities, too. They were very convenient in densely populated cities with great streams of people and covered the intervals from one cross-street to another.

People stood up on spots, gripping handles. Paulo did not hesitate at all and also caught a handle while treading on a blue sidewalk tile. He expected to feel on his face the pleasing puff of the opposing wind, but nothing like this happened. There was no contrary wind, because the ventilation system ensured an air current going in the same direction at the same speed. They had thought about everything.

So, quite unnoticeably, Paulo found himself near the traffic lights. There, stopped at the red light, Dolly was waiting for him. But moving like this was devilish nice! He was much taken with it; he was gleeful, just like a child. Therefore, the youth crossed the street and came up on the opposite sidewalk. Dolly watched him from the car. She had to wait for him at the next crossing.

"Now we have to drive round a little," she said when Paulo got into the car again.

"Why do you need these cars in the city if you have such slides?"

After several turns, in front of them, standing in their way like a Herculean pillar, was the soaring stature of Gallery, and they looked for a place in the underground parking lot. The shopper's dream! One of the famous sights of the city. A mall, which even twenty-five years ago was astounding in both dimensions and capacities.

They bypassed a parking level. It was for electric cars and was crowded. At every parking place, the battery charging devices were hooked up to each car. The parking lot was built on many levels, with modern air-conditioning, and it was able to accommodate dozens of thousands of cars.

The parking places were similar for the other cars, too—those functioning by fuel. After they left the car, the two lovers, embraced, and wended their way—where? To a worship of the god Mercury! This shop, or rather this enormous commerce complex of shops, was incomparable with anything else in the world. It was a temple of commerce. And maybe along with this, a symbol of money. In comparison with its appearance and capacity twenty-five years ago, the trade center was considerably expanded and always remained unsurpassable. Even back then, the word "shop" was losing its meaning here. It went far beyond the scope of such outdated attributes, making them funny. This was a borough of Commodity! Gallery was the first swallow of the development of money and commodity; it was the threshold beyond which one should seriously brood over both money and commodity. Of course, if his consciousness was still not dopey and lulled to sleep by them.

A part of the enormous massive building was located underground, while the visible part of the "iceberg," mostly its top, scattered brilliance—like every iceberg. This effect was due to the roofs—glazed domes allowing a lot of light inside the shop-town. Passing through various "streets," thousands of people were coming in and out of smaller and bigger shops in the huge trade complex. There were winter skating-rinks, toboggan-slides, and skateboard areas; art exhibitions of graphics and modernists; costly restaurants, including panoramic, open-air ones and night clubs; fast food lunch rooms and confectionaries.

And all of this was only some among other things. It was important to see the other things. For it was not the swimming pools and the bowling alleys supporting the trade center, but rather the trade center was supporting them, they were accessories to it. This was a real culture shock in comparison with the living standards of 1989. Life had changed amazingly in only thirty-five years.

Children under sixteen could not cope there unattended. That's why they resorted to the staff's help. Otherwise, they could either damage something or wound themselves somewhere.

Naturally, as always until now, the most interest was in the shops After 2112. Only eighty-eight years left until then, but the maiden flight by pilots to the end of the Solar system instead of the indicated year was already expected to happen much earlier—up to twenty-five or thirty years. So, therefore, the name of the shops could be changed to After 2050. The reason behind this was the revolution in space technologies and especially the creation quite recently of a new space engine gathering a top speed of over thirty-seven-hundred miles per second! The old rockets managed a now funny top speed of only fifteen miles per second. This was a real shock for all of the scientific community, as well as for ordinary people. This was a qualitative leap, not only in space engines but in human development in general. The plans were already to be put into effect in the next ten years for a navigated flight to Jupiter, and maybe even to Saturn! The sensation appeared the next day after receiving the news, the long-awaited happy news, that a human had set foot on Mars. The joy now became double.

Just here, in these shops called After 2112, were offered for sale all of those electronic wonders, which surprised the guest from the past: from the electronic adornments of camouflaged police agents to the ultra-modern video and computer equipment; from sports appliances and facilities to cultural reference works, newspapers and books—all were electronics.

Upon entering at the door, the clients were served by young boys and girls who politely met them, saying, "May I help you? I'm at your service. If you need me, just call me."

On the stalls of each shop, a cornucopia poured out. Slender and young charming girls, always smiling, offered—in fact, guessed—the commodity desired by the client. At one place there was an air humidifier apparatus that was automatic, noiseless, and economical. At another place was a new model of a floating music player, and with its help, the music lover would not have to part with the fancy music, not only on, but also under the water. At a third place was an intelligent set of scales, which congratulated its owner for losing weight or expressed its regret if he put on weight. Near the scales was a dishwashing machine which was also talkative and submitted to vocal commands. The TV sets, carrying out word of commands, too, had exceptionally high definition and were so thin that were hung up as paintings on the walls. This was a miracle unseen forty years ago! Besides that, they had at their disposal the unthinkable earlier ability to receive picture in picture; thus, the good man as a good father could simultaneously watch on the same screen his favorite movie and his beloved child sleeping in the next room.

Along with the ordinary newspapers, which were already dying out, there were also electronic ones on the world web Internet. The electronics were already ousting paper everywhere—in newspapers, books, schedules, etc.

Even the video technology was radically changed. The old video tape and cassette recorders from Paulo's time were long forgotten. The digital video was a qualitatively new technology. Everyone could make films irrespective of the world cinema giants, but mostly using them as home video. Now the digital home video was everywhere through the smart phone—the greatest invention of the computer era! The least used service of the smart phone was its option as a phone. It was everything—pocket computer, radio, TV set, news receiver, camera, a video conversation device, a means of amusement and games, and, finally, a phone, of course.

The cosmetics stall sold the tanning-drops taken by Dolly, as well as various sprays (without Freon, of course), which scattered fragrances that created a pleasant mood, while others were aphrodisiacs intensifying sexual desire.

"You don't need these vials," Dolly said to Paulo. "You aren't in want of either one or the other."

"I agree, darling," Paulo said, giving her an inscrutable smile.

But the most impressive of all was the computers market. There were all kinds of computers: such ones that read a human's mind (the computer already could, while the human mind could not!) and computer-translators the size of old markers that translated immediately upon sliding over written lines. Such pocket personal computers also had other functions. Such PCs were the smart phones, mentioned above—they could connect to databases all over the world and extract the necessary information. That was possible because of the world computer web Internet created on the base of the old world telephone system. The information era for Paulo was like magic and miracles, impossible earlier. Now he could get complete information for everything right off, even for the trifling events and facts—from the first Guinness records to the latest scientific achievements, from information about the first space flight to that about the last Beer Fest.

Maybe the computer had reached its bloom. Passing the stage of the light pen, the modern *touch-screen* technology now allowed the computer to be used just by a finger touching the screen. And this operation turned each computer's owner into a magician! Because of using satellites, it was already possible to make a phone connection between two people who could talk to each other from every nook on the planet, or to locate a man in any moment at any point on Earth and to direct him by using the shortest route possible to an object that interested him.

There was a computer-wreath offered for sale that was put on one's head and enabled direct signals from it to the brain, thus creating images perceived directly to it, much like music from headphones. It was on the same basis as the floating radio that Paulo had seen a little while ago. Using this computer-hoop, one could learn to steer a car, train, or even a plane, as well as train for various sports like skiing, surfing, windsurfing, or yachting, and without any risk.

The computer had come a long way in music, too, even ousting the composer. Everyone who hummed some tune got a written music sheet of a finished melody from the computer, and if it was necessary, the computer printed it. Thus, everyone could be a composer. Actually, the benefit from the computer was the fact that it obviated the composer's fatiguing writing. But nevertheless, there were no great composers yet—whether just because they did not write their notes on their own?

The computers even superseded men in their business. They could conduct merchant negotiations up to some medium-size bargains. After switching in between parties and reaching a decision, the computers then concluded agreements. *You see*, Paulo thought it over, *this computerized already economy is a remote prototype, only the first cursory ray, the rudimentary version of that relieved from men self-organizing, automatic economic system of Omeron, which was realized by androids there. Also, the all-pervading and all-powerful domestic computer in every home is only the prototype of that artificial intelligence, which was situated there in every „cell," and which also attended to everything in it.*

The engineers who demonstrated the capacities of these computers quite kindly explained the necessity that imposed their use, something that, once more, substantiated the youth's thoughts of a little while ago. Because of the laws of competition during the new century, there was already a new way to structure business establishments—the netlike, ensuring elasticity, a lightning reaction to the market changes with only one aim—survival. These economic, netlike structures could become, *under certain conditions*, the evolutionary outset of that perfect production mechanism carried out without payment, without money. For that purpose, the banks' computerization contributed greatly. On each floor of the trade center, as well as everywhere in the city, there were twenty-four-hour, completely automated banks with automatic terminal devices, which served to change and draw out currency, which made the need for a teller quite redundant. So, everywhere in the developed economically world, the unmanned technologies advanced in a mighty and imperative way—in production, in banks, and in trade. Still, at the end of the bygone century, many completely unmanned plants were constructed, mostly in car production. Then this automation came into banks and bank transactions. Now, a few months ago, in the current year of 2023, full automation in trade had begun. In Japan, in the five main supermarket chains, the first completely automated shops without salesmen were introduced. A special chip with barcode on the wares' packing read the price instantly in an automatic cash register, directly from the market basket. After five seconds, the cash register gave change for money, if needed, and a robot arranged the purchases into the market bag. All was in a perfect order.

Obviously, Earth's civilization at this stage followed Omeron's footsteps in its evolution. Once again Paulo thought that what he was seeing on Earth in the technological aspect was a rudimentary, primary state of Omeron's perfect civilization. He remembered Speax's words that the automation in production had led to an unmanned, automatic economy, and the automation in trade to buying orders only at home. "The former eliminated the need for workers, the latter, the need for shops." So, that was the coming future.

Paulo was dizzy from all this diversity. He was fed up with seeing all of this. Finally, he did not even pay serious attention to various computers, which could be folded up like handkerchiefs, crumpled, rolled up, and, in general, deformed in every way without damage.

The guest from the past saw a soft armchair and headed toward it. Dolly had just gone in to her hairdresser, which meant that she wouldn't come out soon. They welcomed Paulo to wait for her here. Sinking into the armchair, Paulo relaxed, expecting certain solitude. But right then a girl appeared from behind his back, one of those slender and appetizing girls who were everywhere here and cared that not a hair of a client's head be hurt. She accosted him with her nice, soft voice to predispose him in her favor. "To get the best rest possible, this chair is just for you. Please, put your feet on the stand below. Here are some headphones, too. Close your eyes, draw a deep breath, and relax entirely. What do you prefer in music?"

This armchair also served as a massage chair. The stand and the arm supports began to gently vibrate. All limbs became as if lighter from this procedure. Through the chair's covering on Paulo's back there stirred small rollers that picked up the circulatory system precisely in those spots where he felt pain from the stored tension after a strain. It was extremely enjoyable.

"I see your endeavor, miss. But I don't intend to buy the chair. Is it possible, however, to stay in it for a while yet?"

"Of course, why not?" The girl smiled back and went off. "Excuse me."

Paulo decided to fill up his time testing his new acquisition—the illusions machine, a home game console, the latest generation. He had bought this plaything a little while ago, and now started to try it out. Therefore, he stood up and went to the hall catering to such functions. Paulo pulled on the helmet and suit of special clothes, switched the console on, and … sank into another, unreal world— the world of the illusions, of electronic "reality," of interactive virtual reality movies.

It was as if he was located in Brazil again. But no, no, these trees and bushes and these crooked animals, ferocious beasts, were as if from another planet. Their appearance frightened him. Here they were. They advanced on all sides with crooked by fury muzzles—gluey, slobbery, nasty. They wanted him, wretch that he was. They stretched out their paws with bloodthirsty yellow or red eyes, and huge sharp tusks from which dirty mucus flowed down. Disgusting monsters, they wanted his soul. Run, run, Paulo!

He rushed forward with all his might. The lad was falling, picking himself up. Bushes and branches were lashing his face across. He was ramming at trees and various little animals. Run, run! Still, still, do you hear? But where? There were more and more coming nearer, and he was overtaken by them. He became sore, exhausted, and completely lost his strength; he stumbled over a hole, and fell on his face. From all directions, beasts of prey with omnifarious degenerate forms were just going to rip him up when, at that moment, he saw an enormous knotty branch nearby. The instinct of self-preservation made him grab the branch as if a samurai's sword and, by a last-ditch effort, to swipe out in self-defense. And then the miracle occurred. Only now did it dawn on Paulo that he could alter everything on his own in this "reality."

With a freezing roar, the nearest monster covered all over in blood, broke forth suddenly and splashed all around, even on Paulo. He swiped again and again, dozens of times, shouting lustily, "I won't give my soul to the Devil!" Heads, limbs, blood, flesh, and bones were flying around until at last all was hushed. The nightmare ended.

This game was obviously created for brave electronic stalwarts, for home supermen, or for megalomaniacal heroes ready to fight evil; but at home, in their slippers.

The next game was the exact opposite. This was God's Eden. Motley birds warbled everywhere amongst fresh greenery, blue sky and light, a lot of light. Their carols floated in the azure of the heavenly spheres among light and bland breezes, soothing the senses. Paulo felt weak, too weak. He could not, and did not want to stir. He hovered in a pink cloud, immovable, wrapped in its blanket. The cloud passed with ease through some palace, through its walls, and took him off to a magnificent royal bedroom suite, whose curtains of light-blue Chinese silk fell immediately after Paulo was laid upon the bed. And all around him revolved calmly, while a voice repeatedly whispered to him, "This is your world. This is your happy world. Forget everything else. Here you are happy, in peace and harmony. This is your world."

The program ended. The dream ended. Paulo stood for a moment and felt heaviness in his head. Then everything became clear. He lifted the headpiece up and pulled it off, as if he had relieved his head from the Egyptian captivity. Suddenly, he turned into the computer hall. The youth stood for a while, aghast. He had a shock at the acceptance of this first dose of dope. "The drugs create tranquility, the police— security," he remembered Khoren's words. Really, what tranquility these new drugs could create!

Indeed, as a training device for pilots, this computer system was wonderful, as a teaching machine for individual tuition in some branch of knowledge, even as a visual electronic system instead of a phone. Okay, but for anything else? A fine drug, truly. Not for nothing, still, at its appearance this plaything was called "electronic LSD." As narcotics were used in medicine for the good of man, these electronic appliances served the same purpose. But they could be of service for his evil, too, as narcotics. Just like them, they led to "emancipation," to breaking up the "fetters" of the existing reality. Only when a man is an outcast from his own reality, from real life, does he look for salvation and solace in another, artificial, sham reality.

The rusticity of the first models from thirty years before had already been removed. In other words, the virtual, the fictitious reality differed in no way from the real, genuine one. For this purpose, the technical difficulties, which initially faced them, were already solved. The two TV monitors had become much smaller, like binocular eyepieces, with exceptional high-definition screen images. Along with them, the headpiece had also become much smaller and lighter with a beautiful form. Also invented was the coveted graphic software that rendered clarified, neat images. And mostly, the computers had become rather more powerful, enabling prompt reactions for changes of the picture according to the player's motions.

What an illusory world! You're asleep and dreaming, you're awake and dreaming again! And thus every day passes—in a ceaseless dream. This is not my world! This is another world!

Paulo made as if to slam the helmet down to the floor. The human soul's revolt! But he refrained. He dragged the headpiece out, and, in the meantime, an attendant came. The young man did not know that during all this time he was being watched. The attendant respectfully accosted him, "Something's wrong, sir? Have you a dislike of the program?"

"Yes," retorted Paulo, "I have a dislike. I dislike *such* a program!"

And he took in the helmet and the suit, went hurriedly up to the refuse can, and dumped these electronic armors as if they were waste matter, useless bric-a-brac. In this matter, he had perceived the immediate danger of repeating in the Solar system the Phaethon's case, of its destructive variant on native soil.

Paulo came out feeling in the dumps.

"What's up? What's wrong with you? Why are you late?" Dolly overwhelmed him with uneasy questions.

"Have you been waiting for me a long time?"

"No, but I didn't find you here, and I thought something unpleasant may have happened to you."

"What could happen? I came back like a bad penny. Come on, let's go."

Dolly was fascination itself with her new hairstyle, but Paulo barely took heed of her. Yet, he was smiling at her. He endeavored not to fall into the role of boring grumbler in her presence. She didn't deserve that.

The pair of lovers got into the car and drove away. Paulo didn't want to go home.

"Why don't we visit Manuel? Anyway, for a long time I've wanted to take a closer view of his work."

"Righto, but only if he's not very busy."

Shortly after they came out from the parking lot, their car skirted along a massive cylindrical installation that the foreigner's eyes had seen in other places of the city, too, and that they would see again by Manuel's institute. This was a small atomic reactor for daily wants, besides it was also used for electricity power production, for example, for warming the water of the local heating system, and it was usually situated near homes or populated public works. In all districts of each city there were such reactors, which were dug in the ground and had safety defenses. This installation was thirty-six feet in height and eighteen feet in diameter. It heated more than two million cubic yards of water per hour up to one-hundred-eighty-five degrees Fahrenheit. An industrial accident was impossible. The possibility was completely excluded because the reactor ran at comparatively low temperatures, the water was not under pressure, and radioactive vapor was not able to come out. And the radiation was very low, as little as from an X-ray apparatus.

Indeed, this was a wonderful present, the result of technical revolution's fruits that created a super industrial society. This was a dream world for the people of the twentieth and especially of the nineteenth centuries. The philosophers of that time had built various enchanting utopias that, in technical aspects, were now far surpassed. But in social aspects, the world was still five thousand years out of step. That is why Paulo was somewhat sad.

He had already rummaged the Internet and had learned many interesting facts. Still, famine was rampant and oppressive social strata existed in the world. Not everyone could afford everything. Violence and injustice still dominated the world, although somewhere, they say, a campaign has started to eradicate them. Really? This would be the greatest achievement of humankind! A society without soldiers, but society of scientists! This was, with certainty, the only way of survival and prosperity for a society. Why should it not be Earth's? Should the man as a wreath of Nature lay a wreath on his own tombstone?

"If the advanced countries," the World Bank's chancery said, not for the first time, "draw in their military expenditures by ten percent, they could double their financial assistance to the developing and poor countries." If! But in comparison to 1990, the poverty in the world had not decreased along with the increase of the world wealth. On the contrary, poverty had grown. It was not just a fourth, but now a third of Earth's population living in poverty, although the standard of living had risen. Three billion people out of nine billion inhabitants of Earth had great difficulty making ends meet. Still, in 1990, there were one-hundred-fifty-seven billionaires and two million millionaires in the world, while at the same time, one-point-two billion people lived in poverty, and one hundred million of them were homeless! Still then! Now the precipice had gone deeper, the cleft had widened and was in danger of turning into a crater. But why did the scientists run away from these facts? Maybe because they were not part of those three billion? What did their apathetic, sideways watching lead to? To Jesus's descent for the second time? Could He do those things that were their duty to do on their own? And should He? This world—of violence and terror, of injustice and wrongs—was doomed to be on its way out. But how? It would either have to perish or to grow forth a new blossom—as a leaf's bud, as a Morello- or apple-blossom. If not, it was worth the end.

At last, man had to understand with all his fiber (not the electronic ones, of course!), at last man had to fathom that the source of all Earth's misfortunes and evils in society were due to the State with its energy system—money! Each state serves the dissociation of people: inside it, of classes; outside it, of nations. And only in this is the highest injustice in any society—the robbery, the exploitation of particular people and of whole peoples, its division into poor and rich, into servants and masters. From here on, violence comes on its own. It is only an effect of social injustice. They are both the most important features that determine the nature of the State, features that form the outlines of the State. All others boil down to these. From its nascency, the State is an ultimate, final phase of organized criminality. So many people on Earth do not understand that, in its present makeup, the State is a criminal organization. Not only because its rulers take part in malfeasances right along through unceasing machinations, corruption, and underhanded games—this is only the effect; but simply because mostly its own existence morally outlaws it; its own existence is a crime towards the enormous part of its citizens, because it oppresses them in different ways. It is a crime toward the poor: once, because it robs them and turns them into poor, and second, because it keeps them poor, because it reproduces them poor, both in particular people and in whole peoples. And besides that, the State kills! In every way and in everything! So, if private property is theft, the State's existence is a crime against personality.

Why was the State necessary under the conditions of this so-developed, yet social organization of production and consumption? Why was the State necessary under the conditions of this so well-developed social self-regulation? Maupassant was, with certainty, right that the State is the same old stupidity set in might and authority. But who still reads in this electronic society? The illiterates were on the increase, the foolish still more. After the UNO specialists in the year 2000, nine-hundred-fifteen-million people over the age of fifteen were illiterate. The illiteracy in men amongst otherwise highly intelligent robots grew incessantly. If in 1985 there were a hundred and five million illiterate children, in 2000 there were two hundred million, and in 2020 there were already about four hundred million!

Meanwhile, evidence for foolish men had not been revealed. Not because it was not possible. It was thus accepted. But it would be a good practice to keep such statistics, too. Perhaps it should issue a separate bulletin for them, of another report: *Register Stultitia.*

Some robots already looked at themselves in a mirror, recognized themselves, and were liked. Just like Isaac Asimov's robots. The day was not far away when artificial men would pop up. Their mass production was only a question of time—in up to forty or fifty years they would be already a new humanoid race taking possession of all the rest! But anyway through the new technologies and existing social and economic system of capitalism, natural men turned into artificial ones, why then should not the artificial men begin to resemble the natural ones? Still, in 2017, the European Union's statesmen discussed providing "human rights" to robots. Really! It was not madness or a sci-fi fable! Still then, this process of substitution of natural men with artificial ones has begun.

Paulo sat thoughtfully in the car and looked outside with unseeing eyes. He did not even notice that they had already reached their destination and that the car had stopped.

"Why so silent? I don't know you like this," Dolly questioned him.

"Nothing, I'm thinking. Things are all so confusing."

"Which things?"

"Well, all." Smiling Paulo decided to fib, dissembling his real thoughts. "My mother has become the age of my grandma, while my sister is at her own place. Manuel is as though he's not my cousin but my uncle. And his daughter, instead of being my niece, is my lover!"

Paulo embraced her tenderly, smiled as before, and kissed her.

"You see, don't you? All is not as it should be," he added.

"On the contrary, all is as it should be. Because I love you."

"Be in no hurry to say these words. They aren't for day-to-day use."

"But I love you! Really!"

They got out of the car and, at that moment, noticed that, not far from them, Manuel was talking with some businessman in the park. This was a trim garden with skillfully arranged alleys. There were many flowers, as well as various fresh birches, firs, oaks, spruces, and other trees. All of the trees had been made by test-tube. Through this method, they got increased hardiness towards harmful changes in the environment, they grew faster, and it was possible to produce them in larger quantities than under natural cultivation.

The two men parted, and Manuel set out for the building's entrance. Then Paulo and Dolly, who had already started toward him, beckoned him, and he stopped. The three went up to his study.

"You're coming just in time, as if I've placed an order. Please, settle yourselves," Manuel said, gesturing them to their seats. "Do you know, I considered talking with you this evening, Paulo." He ceased speaking for a moment, looking at Dolly, too. "Actually, with both of you. I know about you. I mean, I've become aware of things."

"What things have you become aware of?" Paulo asked.

"Your relationships with Dolly." And on "uncle" Manuel's mouth, a smile emerged.

"And you find no harm in that?"

"No. Why? You're still twenty-four. Besides that, even a blind man can see in your eyes the 'Ode to Joy' when you are together and alone."

"Well, okay. I'll be your cousin, nephew, and son-in-law simultaneously. You can call me what you want. You'll have many relatives together at one place, especially if a grandchild is born."

"Wonderful! That means we'll celebrate in a family circle his or her first cry on the Moon!"

"What? Where?" Dolly jumped up.

"On the Moon. Maybe you've heard about it."

"Wait, wait … wait for a minute." Paulo jumped up, too. "Baby? The Moon? What does that mean, Manuel? In fact, 'uncle'! And perhaps 'Dad'? I have no near plans for one or the other. The baby is as far to me as the Moon. Besides that, what are you talking about, baby on the Moon? How could you think that?"

"Well, this is what I mean. I saw that you have anxiety about looking at Earth from the Moon, Paulo, at least for a while. But you see, it opened up a chance to take you with me on the *Biosphere 3* Program. Therefore, I intended to suggest this participation to you and thought to have a talk this evening only with you. But when I saw you both just now, the cracked idea flashed on me to take you together. Yes, why not? It will be good for you. It will be good for the program, as well. Its significance will grow quite unexpectedly, abruptly, and still more. No one has yet done this. We're always talking about a settlement there, but we're still only immigrants. There's not one born lunar man. There's not one native moon inhabitant. And on the other side, I'm sure that Dolly won't leave you to go anywhere alone. She'd set right off out after you anywhere, even in the remotest corner of the world, even on the Moon, let's say. Is that so, Dolly?"

"Yes, Dad," she answered somehow bashfully.

"So, if you both wish, you could come as participants in the program that, in this way, we'll enrich with research. Not much is known yet about sex in the cosmos, and we have no experience with the maternity process. Although it has long been known that conception in space is possible, as Japanese scientists proved back in 2017. We know also that the Moon is ideal for underground preservation of sperm."

"But this is such a risky enterprise! What if something went wrong? How will he or she breathe there? And what if it is born injured or subsequently degenerated? This will be a baby of mine, Dad! Of *mine!* And to let it be a test rabbit? No, no, I disagree." The girl shuddered at the thought.

"I know, Dolly. And the baby will be a grandchild of mine, too. I also don't want anything wrong to befall our child. But don't worry. The conditions inside this base are identical to those on Earth. Artificial gravitation is created, thanks to superconductivity, and man weighs there just as much as he weighs on Earth. The soil inside under the glass-cover differs in no way from Earth's dirt—it's even better. And the air is a hundred times clearer even than that of the freshest virgin forest or of the clearest mountain peak here such as they were not long ago, by the way. So, the baby will breathe! And it will even run along waterfalls and lianas, just like Tarzan. The child won't be in danger even of allergens. And besides that, physicians, some of the best specialists, will constantly keep watch over the kid. It will enjoy such respect and attention you won't find anywhere else. I'm also very cautious in this respect, and we have to think about a number of more things."

"I'm not sure, Dad," Dolly continued to be confused.

"Okay, okay. You'll make a decision. No one will bind you in any way. There are still three months until then. The program will take just two and half years, just thirty months.

"Well, righto," Paulo joined in the chat. "I'm just going to save my inconveniences and your assets by those one hundred thousand dollars for the ticket to the Moon. But I thought to enroll at the university. You understand, don't you? The never-ending student. And I even had a plan to move into a hostel in a few days."

"But your studies are not a problem at all from the Moon either. You'll be able to attend lectures or exams from there by means of television … I mean, through a video-phone system. You'll be able to see the professor as if you are in the same room."

"Yes, I know this system. For educational work it maybe is excellent, but for something else … Actually, when will you acquaint me with your job? What computers are you working with now? I see that here, on Earth, each box teaches you some sense. I see that everything has begun to speak. I just don't know whether the scientists' conscience did, too –"

"What do you mean?"

"Well, I mean whether they still create new weapons for their old thinking?"

"We turn the weapons more and more toward the space invaders, the asteroids, but unfortunately, we still keep them directed between us, as well. We built a space shield, a cosmic guard of laser systems against unexpected, unforeseen asteroids coming near and ready to collide with us. This was as a result of a sobering event in July 1999 when an asteroid barely concussed Earth. Only then did we realize our mistake that it is one-for-all, and we turned some of the *Star Wars* Program's guns towards these intruders. It's a pity that we didn't do it earlier."

"Oh, you could talk no end until tomorrow, but I'm having a dull time with this," Dolly broke in, displeased.

"In that case, if you're bored, you can go home if you want. Both of us will stay on and come back together in my car," Manuel suggested, and then saw her out the door after she took her leave of Paulo.

Meanwhile, Paulo looked round and only then noticed the study's windows. They were made by electro-steerable glasses, i.e., windows with electro-steerable coloration of the glasses. That meant that it was piled up in many exceptionally thin layers, a lamellar covering that changed its color according to the magnitude of the electric tension flowing through it. Thus, the windows were able to take on the appearance from transparent to one color or multi-colored like the windows in a Gothic cathedral. They were different and more functional than the electronic window-pictures such as he saw on the train during his travels here. There were such windows in his hosts' house, too.

Paulo cast a look at the furniture, as well. It seemed that everywhere was modern the upholstered one with artificial leather differing in no way from the natural one and which was covered by holographic pictures in various motifs. But he did not see them, because this view lasted a very short time, since Manuel came back at that moment and resumed his explanation.

"When we're speaking of the lasers in space as a shield, as a guard, I have to tell you that they're the crowning achievement of Earth's science. These are free-electron lasers. They're able to be tuned with ease, gradually in different wavelengths, from one end to the other of the spectrum, and they have smashing power at minimum energy consumption, up to a thousand terawatts and up to one hundred percent efficiency!"

"I hope the military won't turn these lasers on people. They could become awful, super mighty annihilating weapons, couldn't they?"

"Well, that's true, but I hope things won't come to such a development. However, I see that you are seriously anxious about the good of mankind. This thought has corralled you." Paulo's "father-in-law" held his eyes on him. "Now, come, I want to show you something."

Manuel unlocked the door of a neighboring room by touching a fingerprint sensor.

"Look." He pointed at a not large transparent box. "This is the greatest achievement of the computer era! The light computer! Look at this. Instead of silicon chips and panels, there are lasers, lenses, and mirrors. Instead of the old electronic processor, there is the optical one. Instead of millions of operations per second, there are billions of them! The optical computer works thousands of times faster than the fastest electronic computers. It finds exceptionally wide applications. It is used for processing information coming in from the biggest particle accelerator for mastery of thermonuclear synthesis. It is priceless for deciphering human DNA's structure in every detail. This computer is a part of those seeing-robots that must recognize images in the automated workshops of the plants for specialized activities, such as fitting details together, transportation, delivery, and the like. And at length, the light computer is one of the most important components in lots of systems for our expedition to Mars. And it's the most complex and expansive program Earth's scientists have ever implemented."

"And what do you think about that shocking report of a space engine enabling a top speed of three-thousand-seven-hundred-fifty miles per second?"

"This is subject to serious verification! And if it proves to be true, this is super sensational. Can you imagine? A flight to Titan in less than three days! Fantastic!"

"Titan, Saturn's satellite? Why, is there something special there?"

"Since, as many scientists think, Titan is the most hospitable to man's astronomical body in the Solar system after Earth. Titan's environment is much better than that of Mars. The atmospheric pressure on Titan is a bit higher than Earth's, and this allows the explorers there to work without space suits. They will only need warm clothes and oxygen masks. The curse of Mars—the radiation—because of which earth men must live deeply beneath its surface, does not exist on Titan, and, at the moment, this is its main priority over Mars. Besides that, beneath the surface of Titan there is much more water than on Mars. Yet, my favorite planet remains Mars. Imagine if we have this space engine, the flight to Titan will be less than three days, while Mars will be only eleven or twelve hours from us!"

Manuel was enthusiastically talking, and Paulo was listening with interest. Especially close to Manuel's heart was the march to Mars. The Martian Chronicles had begun in 1992, when the *Mars Observer* spacecraft had blasted off to the red planet in order to study its surface, atmosphere, climate, and magnetic field. Unfortunately, this mission failed, but four years later it was supervened by the *Mars Global Surveyor* with full success. Thanks to this mission, a global mapping of the entire planet was completed in 2001, from the ionosphere down through the atmosphere to the surface. It has been a great success, although this spacecraft's connection was lost after ten years of good work. The next successful Martian project was *Curiosity*. This rover landed in 2012 as a part of the *Mars Science Laboratory* mission. *Curiosity* has continued to study the climate of Mars, as well as its geology, the role of water there, and to collect useful information for the future manned-mission to the red planet.

For the exhausting space marathon to Mars, wasteless technologies have been necessary. Therefore, a new species of fly has been genetically invented, for example, that, after laying its eggs, the hatched maggots fed on the wastes in the spacecraft's closed system. They have transformed the wastes into rich, clear humus, on which vegetables like tomatoes, cucumbers, and mushrooms could be planted. A part of the maggots have used as food for the quails bred by the astronauts as delicacies to their menu.

After a period of stagnation and marking time in the space exploration, in 2019 it tested an unmanned variant of the spacecraft *Pegasus*, and in 2022 *Pegasus* itself started. It has had a total initial mass of three hundred and forty-five tons and has been fit together by only a few plies of the shuttle. The flight's program has included six hundred and one days going, two hundred and sixty-eight days returning, and one hundred days of exploration work. Until this moment it was running a week out from the exploration work.

The engine of *Pegasus* has had only five tons of mass ejecting ionized gas with a speed of fifty miles per second at an efficiency of forty percent. The gas-working substance has been one hundred tons of liquid argon, and the electric supply has been realized by a nuclear reactor. The Russians have designed a similar engine, with one difference—instead of argon as the working substance, they used xenon. In general, the Russians also have had ambitious plans for scientific exploration of Mars, but those were mostly on paper only. The reason has been the Second Cold War between Russia on one hand, and the United States and European Union on the other. All scientific elaborations for Mars's research with balloons and rovers have been stopped in Moscow, while, at the same time, NASA has managed to implement three new missions from 2003 on. *Spirit*, *Opportunity*, and *Curiosity* were triumphs of Earth science and the human spirit. However, it became more and more clear that only the joint endeavors of a great many states could lead to much more successful exploration of the near cosmos. And this imposed the need for unification of humanity, of all of Earth's civilization into a united and mature society in the name of its advance and welfare.

NASA was making enormous strides in cosmic space. Its engineers had designed the next stupendous project—*Parker Solar Probe*. It was the latest generation probe, a robotic spacecraft the size of a small car launched in order to "touch" the Sun, to probe our star's outer corona. Dispatched in the summer of 2018, it would have approached to within less than ten solar radii (that means 4.3 million miles) from the center of the Sun to its "surface" (the photosphere) in 2025. As the probe passed around the Sun, it would have achieved a velocity of up to one hundred and twenty miles per second, making it by any measure the fastest manmade object ever. It had various scientific goals, such as determining the structure and dynamics of the magnetic fields at the sources of solar wind; tracing the flow of energy that heats the corona and accelerates the solar wind; determining what mechanisms accelerate and transport the energetic particles; and the very important goal of exploring the dusty plasma near the Sun and its influence on solar wind and energetic particle formation.

At the very same time, there were feverish preparations for the *Ulise* program. A flight to the Sun of the *Ulise 1* craft was planned for the next 2024. And in 2039, at least in theory, it was expected there'd be *Ulise 5*, too, a manned mission to the Sun like a new Icarus, the greatest triumph of the untamable human spirit.

19

Paulo looked at the calendar on the wall. The date was November 21, 2029. By now, six months had passed since they moved into their new place. Many things in it bore a resemblance to Eden. Paulo and Dolly lived here and felt just like Adam and Eve, although there were other people around them, too. Yet, in a sense, they really were the lunar Adam and Eve. The mission included eight people—scientists, engineers, technicians—who had to develop this lunar settlement so that after ten years its residents already would be a hundred people.

A variety of reasons retarded their project for six years—more financial, less technical—but in the last reckoning, the mission was realized. The young family had been living on the Moon for half a year already. Beneath the dome of *Biosphere*, the two lunar inhabitants were living their experimental life as biblical people amongst a primeval forest, caroling birds, babbling brooks, and rills and cascades, all of them flowing into unruffled ponds. Earth paradise on the Moon! But if there is death in paradise, its name is boredom. Their time until now, however, did not drag. They had to do so many research projects. Anything else, but not boredom. Besides that, they partook in the ceaseless information interchange with Earth in the twenty-four-hour programs of several world TV channels. Earth knew them and kept up with them as well as they kept up with it.

Their project would have to be one of the last where sex was used for family continuation in the natural way. If soon the existing social and economic system of capitalism would not be changed, then with certainty the people would be changed! In the most developed countries, a process of creation of a new human race by artificial means had begun. In special laboratories the first "designer babies" were custom-made. The expectations were that after ten or twenty years, towards 2040–2050, mankind's reproduction would take place only through high technologies, while sex would remain only for pleasure, for amusement, something like a hobby. Offspring would have to be set up in an artificial way, while sex for reproduction will have become an anachronism and would disappear. The children will not have that value they have always had for hundreds and thousands of years earlier in human history. The family will have died out and instead of it, the man and woman would not be parents, but only partners—a couple for the production of children: the man gives up sperm, and the woman a piece of skin. And that's all, designer babies are made. What a dark future for the artificial people! For that reason, Paulo and Dolly's project was such an important alternative. Japanese scientists proved long ago, still twelve years ago, that conception in space is possible and that the Moon is a perfect place for underground preservation of sperm.

The space near the planet-mother was very settled. When Paulo and Dolly were coming to the Moon, they also saw in orbit, along with the multitude of satellites, space stations with various purposes. There were some with production activities. On them were thermonuclear systems that produced cooling rays protecting Earth from calorific overheating and the greenhouse effect. There were other space stations in the tourist business. Hotels were situated in low orbit for space tourism—American, Japanese, and Chinese. For example, the first hotel, *Aurora Space Station*, the American pioneer of this business, from 2022 received only four guests out of two pilots' crews, while the Japanese hotel, *New Otani Space*, the next generation's hotel, from 2028 received up to forty visitors, paying the price for a "night's lodging," i.e., five twenty-four-hour periods, at two hundred thousand dollars per person, a price much lower than nearly eight hundred thousand dollars for a "night's lodging" in *Aurora*. The hotel was a cylinder, as were all the rest, in fact, which was eight hundred feet long and four hundred and fifty feet in diameter, rotating around its axis with three revolutions per minute for the purpose of obtaining artificial gravitation.

Actually, the Japanese had penetrated everywhere, not only into space. They built cities over and below the earth, over and below the water. They tried to outdo each other in raising towers in the air. Hard pressed by the unimaginable prices of land, the Japanese were forced to work wonders. They fought for each inch of land, each drop of water, each sip of air. After the initial project for a skyscraper was built for one hundred and thirty-two thousand people, stretching three thousand feet high and named Sky City, a second one immediately appeared with a height of sixty-six hundred feet, and almost right beside it, a project of a pyramid soaring up to thirteen thousand feet in the sky! This imposing mountain was completed only a year ago, and with eight hundred floors was home to seven hundred thousand people! Weren't they all distant portents of those hyper megalopolises without any peer, beyond any imagination—the hanging cities-*glial cells*, on Omeron? There were quite a few similarities. Both there and here, each city's floor was on automatic controls for almost all parts. Both there and here, each floor of each such city possessed its own power-plant, its own purifying sewage installations, and its own communication systems. And certainly the Japanese engineers' experience for counteraction and drive against the frequent and strong earthquakes through softening junctions would have enabled the future builders to create those cities-cosmopolises flexibly connected between themselves in the air.

In contrast to the cities-megalopolises, in Japan there existed also underground cities-*molehills* that represented complex engineering and technical cupola installations. They had, as with all normal cities, shops, power-plants, gardens, parks, offices, hotels, restaurants, railroads, and waste-recycling plants and were situated between one hundred and fifty and two hundred and fifty feet under the surface. The construction of these nets of underground cities, like ant-hills, in which the Japanese swarmed just like industrious ants, had lasted twenty years. It was lasting now, too.

In search of living space in the ocean, the ingenious Japanese had created cities-islands. Each one of them was borne by ten thousand pillars treading on the bottom on concrete blocks at a depth of six hundred and fifty feet, and towering two hundred and seventy feet above the water. These artificial islands were safely protected against tsunamis, earthquakes, and high tides. Transportation to the short distances between them was realized by hovercraft as well as water-air taxies.

And as an acme of the constructional engineering genius, the Japanese had created subaqueous industrial towns. It was again because of the exceptional want of space. One such subaqueous town consisted of five hundred tunnels, each one of which was ten miles long, a hundred feet high, and sixty-six feet wide. Each town's total area was an average of ninety-five square miles. In the tunnels, on many floors, there were built and situated on each floor various plants, completely automated and robotized; there were multitudes of stores of prime and raw materials, as well as finished products, garages, halls, and a number of other rooms.

As he was sitting in impatient expectation of the great event and looking at the moonscape and Earth out there, Paulo was thinking, floated by his memories. The childbirth had still not begun.

At that moment, he overheard the clear sound of the bell that called all the group's members to lunch. It was Ferry, the robot. It was a robot-cook and along with this a waiter, too. Each space or sea ship, each expedition, including the Martian one, had at least one such robot. At a fixed time, at a fixed hour, he opened the refrigerator, took out ready-made foods, and put them into a microwave oven to warm them up. After all was ready, by pressing a bell, Ferry called the hungry astronauts, working up to this moment, to sit down around the table.

The space foods were prepared by sublimation, a drying process. The astronauts especially liked the Bulgarian tarator—the summer "white cold soup," as the Americans called it. In the first years of space flights, because of weightlessness, wine and cognac were not drunk, but were eaten in the form of pills.

The same with bourbon. Such "medicine" was taken only after the end of the working day, and in insignificant quantities. However, here, in *Biosphere 3*, under the same living conditions as on Earth, they could take the liquids normally, i.e., drink them. Now, after many years of experience in the International Space Station and many numbers of space flights, the astronauts began their working day with cups of Chinese herbal tea or Italian espresso Lavazza. Lunch could be Bulgarian tarator, Russian borsch, or Japanese sushi, and supper included over two hundred dishes like yuxiang pork, dried beef, or chicken garnished with various salads and racy sauces.

Besides that, Ferry offered food of its own design, mainly vegetables—onions, tomatoes, radishes, cucumbers, carrots and the like—by which it made three salads for each person per week at four-member service groups. And there were eight people.

Paulo stayed on to wait. He shifted his eyes and they fell on the digging robots. They needed neither food, nor wine, still less cognac or bourbon. They dug ditches and laid pipes into them, through which they stretched various cables. And they made everything on their own. Thinking machines.

The robots were everywhere. They were quietly conquering the world. They were speaking, hearing, seeing. The robots had artificial muscles, the first of which, although slower, were much stronger than the human ones—they lifted loads hundreds of times heavier than man could. But later, coming in large numbers, were the robots with muscles made by polymer gel. The humanoid robots began more and more to resemble man. And they began more and more to oust him, everywhere, in everything. They were cooks, cleaners, divers, pilots, surgeons, geologists, artists, musicians, technicians detecting leaks on planes and spacecraft fuselages, and what not. Not far off was the day when they would have to launch their own labor-unions! And this was not a joke, but a real opportunity after these robots long ago got the statute of humans and, respectively, "human rights."

Another direction of the robots' development was the integral micromechanics. These were midget, microscopic robots exercising various functions. For example, the micro robots could clean the hurtful build-up of collagen on the eyes' retina; to clean the arteries from sclerosis's lodged lumps, as well as all kinds of impassable or difficult to access places in the human body. These "sanitary outfits" were taken in ordinary tablets, in the form of "reasoning" pills. So, this new pharmacy considerably prolonged man's life.

Thanks to the robots, it became possible to do something that earlier was not even thinkable—a surgeon operating from a distance! The surgery had already achieved fantastic successes. The transplantation of various organs was already a routine procedure, especially after the phenomenal success of a transplantation of a head! Now the rich could live forever, changing his or her body every twenty years! Besides this, the regenerative medicine was already in a position to cultivate a whole heart under laboratory conditions! Because of medicine's phenomenal successes, personal health became a cult for everyone who could afford it in his or her aspiration for immortality.

So, distant operations were not an exception yet. It happened so that such an operation was performed here quite recently.

Two of the astronauts, Pete and Steven, were going out to check on the solar panels. One of them had failed. This was not fatal, of course, because the settlers obtained the energy mainly by the atomic power station nearby. But one way or another, the failure had to be removed.

Before long, however, the two men came back. To be precise, Pete dragged Steven back. For unknown to Pete reason, the air in Steven's spacesuit had run out after a short while. After the third call on his helmet phone, Pete had gone to see what happened to his friend. Steven had slid down lifeless next to one column. Pete had immediately given him a hypobiotic injection and brought him along to the base. Sliding down unconscious, Steven had seriously wounded his head and cervical vertebrae on the bars sticking out around the column. He also had swelling of the lungs. It was necessary to do an emergency operation. Of course, they could give him one more injection, and the hypobiosis would keep him still as was needed, but there were six whole days before the next spacecraft arrived. It was too much time to sit on their hands. But there was not such a specialist on the base. They were missing such a highly skilled surgeon. What then? The only decision left was an operation by a robot. Science had already allowed for that.

They called up one of the best surgeons in the United States, Dr. Glen Murdock. He responded immediately to the request, dropping his other official duties.

The surgeon hurried into the special medicine department of NASA's Mission Control Center in Houston. He established contact with the robot on the Moon that would have to perform the operation through a TV connection. After that, Dr. Murdock put a visor-shaped optical appliance on his head. Through it he could see the operating field. When everything was right, the physician slipped on gloves with electronic sensors in order to operate the robot's lancet. The robot, on its part, incessantly transmitted information about Steven's condition—blood pressure, pulse, internal organs function, temperature, vibrations, and all the rest. All of this was conveyed to the surgeon, transmuted by the sensors into physical sensations in order that Dr. Murdock could actually feel the operation, and thus guide it precisely. And something more, the physician knew perfectly that the signal he received on Earth would be more than a second late, and the feedback more than two seconds late; therefore, he coordinated his gestures taking this delay into account.

The operation was long and hard, but successful. Steven was rescued. And the surgery experienced its triumph, its serial triumph!

In the lunar settlement, all people and robots had gotten into the full swing of work. Really, up to 2040, at least a hundred people would have lived here. They would have built dwellings by 3D printers and melted lunar ice in order to obtain water, and these practices were still being used now, in this mission. It was envisaged in the next missions the settlers would lead a life of full value—in their spare time they would have to visit leisure centers, bars, restaurants, and sports facilities. Using the Moon's weak gravitation, all sorts of competitions and even Olympiads could be organized—some semi-flying sports like lunar track-and-field events, lunar volleyball, basketball, and many others.

As a part of the new moonscape, off in the distance was the 52.5-foot optical infrared telescope that could spot space objects twinkling forty times weaker than those observed up to 1990. The scientists searched planets around other stars. Great successes were achieved in this search much earlier, until 2017, with the Hubble telescope, but with such an imposing telescope on the Moon the progress was now enormous. However, Omeron was still unknown to them.

A parabolic radio antenna with a diameter of nearly five thousand feet was raised in one of the craters. Likewise, a radio interferometer building was forthcoming with a range of almost two hundred and forty thousand miles that would have an immense angular resolution. And towards this, at the present time, the LUISA project was constructed—an interferometer with a hundred thousand times better angular resolution than the existing one until 1990, when this project was sanctioned for the first time. Its antennas were arranged into two concentric circles—thirty-three telescopes ranged in the external six-mile circle and nine telescopes describing the internal circle with a thousand and six hundred-fifty feet in diameter. Probably in the next year, 2030, it would have discovered the Sirius C star.

As continuation of the SETI project from 1974 (the radio signal Arecibo Message to the globular cluster M13), in 1992 NASA had endorsed a search program for radio signals by other civilizations. There fifteen million frequencies were used. The closest six hundred stars were searchingly inquired. And nothing! On Alpha Centauri A, the civilization was only two hundred years backwards, but enough to not be able to send a signal. At this instant, the steam locomotive had hardly given a toot. The industrial revolution had hardly begun there. The radio was just being born, and because of that, the first its signals were still far away in time. Nearly half a century was needed before one James Clerk Maxwell expounded the electromagnetism, including the radio waves, before they could be sent somewhere far away as a message.

And what about 61 Cygni? There was no longer a need for these signals there.

Sirius? It was pointless to search there.

While Paulo was looking outside and thinking during all this time, from somewhere the bewitching music of *Moonlight Sonata* wafted, which had an exceptional effect here. A unique experience! Beethoven could hardly ever have imagined this! Earth had risen as sickle straight ahead. How beautiful it was only! A blue pearl amongst the black space of wilderness! Would someone have to compose the *Earthlight Sonata*?

They called him. The childbirth had begun.

Has it come yet? Paulo thought to himself and stood up.

The first moon baby! The first man on the Moon! *Homo Cosmicus!*

Dolly was delivering in a tub. She seemed very strained, but she still smiled at Paulo the moment she saw him. He went to her and took her hand in his. He stroked her tenderly and with love.

The newest chapter for humankind was being commenced.

The year was 2029. On Earth the waves of a social revolution were sweeping over Europe. On Earth, in Europe, the new man was being born!

"It's born! Born! *Boooorn!*" Paulo yelled with all his might when the physician raised the newborn child in his hands. It roared out vigorously, it began to cry as proof of life, and its first shout as if rang out through the whole Cosmos, as though dinned into the Universe as a mighty organ sound.

Review Requested:

If you loved this book, would you please provide a review at Amazon.com?